ARISE

Book Three of The Syrenka Series

Amber Garr

Arise

Book Three of The Syrenka Series

by Amber Garr

Copyright © 2012 Amber Garr

www.ambergarr.com

This is a work of fiction. The names, characters, places, and incidents are products of the author's imagination or have been used fictitiously and are not to be construed as real. Any resemblance to actual persons, living or dead, events, or locales is entirely coincidental.

All rights are reserved. No part of this book may be used or reproduced in any manner whatsoever without written permission from the author.

Cover Design by PhatPuppyArt

ISBN-13: 978-1477559154
ISBN-10: 1477559159

ACKNOWLEDGEMENTS

Writing and publishing this series has been a wonderful experience, and one that wouldn't have happened without the help of several people. Thank you Celia for shaping this manuscript into a better story and for working your way through it with me. I am excited to see your words in print someday soon. To Andrea, a competent writer yourself, thank you for your edits, comments, and compliments. I look forward to working on a joint project together in the near future (hint hint). For Elizabeth, who has been there since I shared my first short story, thank you for your consistent support, editing skills, and all around excitement for this project. I hope that I can return the favor soon. Thank you Betsy, a new addition to the beta readers, for your fabulous comments and your enthusiasm for the series. I appreciate you taking the time to help complete the final book. To Sandy, thank you for always making my day with your kind words and compliments on my endeavors. To my mom, I know you aren't a huge fan of the supernatural, but you helped review nonetheless, and for that I am grateful. A big thanks to Marisette, Serena, and Carol who are some of the best critique partners in the world. And also to The Palm City Word Weavers who continue to encourage and inspire every day. Finally, I'd like to thank the fans of The Syrenka Series who have enjoyed losing themselves in my world of merfolk and selkies. I thought about you a lot while writing this last book, and I hope your journey with Eviana is one that you'll always remember. Thank you!

AMBER GARR

ONE

Eviana

    I never thought I would beg for death. It simply wasn't my style. I was stubborn and determined, not broken and weak. When life turned against me, I fought back. I never gave up. So why was it so hard for me to open my eyes right now?

    The door creaked open with a groan. A single beam of light catapulted my room into an altogether different landscape. The dark walls were highlighted enough for me to see the intricate ridges and grooves of the coral stones. Skeletons of an ancient reef surrounded me on all four sides of my prison. The irony wasn't lost on me. I was a creature of the sea, trapped by a once living animal now reduced to nothing more than a stone. Its purpose in life stolen away the moment it was removed from its home. Just like me.

    A silhouette of a small woman temporarily blocked the light and I was thrust back into darkness. I'd become accustomed to the dark. It was safe and comfortable and it matched the way I felt inside. Alone and empty.

"*La sirenita?*" a tiny voice called into the shadows of the room. When I didn't answer, she opened the door wider and I threw up my arm to block the light from my eyes. "*Ah, la sirenita. Ven a comer.*"

She placed the plate on the floor and crouched down next to it. Holding out her hand, she beckoned me to come toward her and the fresh food, coaxing me like a stray dog.

"*Venga!*"

I shook my head and turned away from her. We'd been through this numerous times. She would come in, put the plate on the floor, and leave when I refused to acknowledge her existence. As if on cue, I heard her sigh and gather up the uneaten food she'd brought in a few hours earlier. My Spanish was rough, but I swear she mumbled something about me being a stupid little mermaid before slamming the door shut again.

Not long after she'd leave, another stranger would enter the room. He was much larger and smelled like he bathed in dead fish. Although he never spoke to me, I could hear him breathe as if it were difficult for him to use his nose. At first I was scared and would try to fight. But it was always a useless attempt because the moment he got close enough I would feel the prick of the syringe. Within seconds, the world blurred and I'd slip back into an endless coma of sleep and despair.

It was the only routine in my life since I'd been kidnapped by my estranged father. *Estranged* probably wasn't even the right description although I just recently discovered his true identity. Words like *delusional*, *crazy*, or *psychotic* would be a better depiction of the man who killed my parents, my uncle, and my friends along with many others. His insane ideas and extreme behavior created a divide amongst my kind and I would imagine that by now, we were officially at war with one another.

I had been trapped in this room for days. Or at least that was my assumption. The back of my head, where my loving father had knocked me out, still ached. I hadn't been in any water, although I could sense some nearby, so my body was unable to heal quickly.

If I could just get to the water, maybe I could escape. Maybe it would give me the desire to fight against my captors. Each time I got an injection, my will to survive seemed to fade into a haze like my surroundings. I knew that I was being drugged but I couldn't bring myself to care anymore.

When the door squeaked open again, I didn't even bother to acknowledge the large, fish-smelling man. He was right on schedule with his syringe and when he stuck the needle into my shoulder, I felt a tear roll down my cheek. Maybe this would be the last day I had to endure.

But when I opened my eyes to find the tiny Spanish speaking lady changing out my food plate again, I realized that my life wasn't over yet. It took me a few moments before I noticed that she wasn't speaking to me, although she was talking a mile a minute. I could hear the heavy breathing of the fish man who grunted in acknowledgement of her comments.

My brain forced a command through my body to sit up and turn around, but the muscles and bones didn't want to listen. It wasn't until I heard the man's feet shuffle out the door that I was finally able to muster up enough energy to focus on my surroundings.

The woman stood near the doorway, shifting nervously side to side while her attention darted between me and the open door. I almost laughed. It's not like I was in any kind of shape to dash past her, but as long as she thought that way, I wouldn't correct her.

I heard some kind of mumbling from outside and a few seconds later, the light was blocked when two figures entered the room. The woman jumped out of the way as the large man threw a body toward my corner with a little too much force. It thumped and scraped against the hard coral stone causing me to wince in sympathy.

Yet what I heard next made me want to scream in frustration.

"You don't have to be so rough, mate." The perfect British accent sent shivers down my spine and caused my first emotional outburst since I'd been captured.

"What is he doing here?" I tried to shout, even though it came out as a whimper.

Instead of answering, the man and woman chuckled and left me behind with the one person I loathed more than my captor.

"I'm happy to see you too, tart."

Graham. Graham Forrester was locked in this prison with me. He was a Council member, a potential suitor, and an all around traitor to his kind. His alliance with Lucian, my biological father, was what led to my capture in the first place. Despite his brief attempt to help me, the guy didn't have a decent bone in his body.

"Don't call me that," I snapped, imagining the crooked grin on his face. I heard him sliding around on the floor and suddenly the adrenaline pumped through my body. "Stay away from me!"

Before he could respond, the floor began to vibrate. It shook so bad, I was forced to crabwalk backward against the far wall and huddle in the corner. Dust and coral pieces fell to the floor and ricocheted off my fragile body.

It wasn't until I heard the scraping of stone on stone that I raised my head to see the floor literally splitting apart down the center of the room. The moment the crack appeared, I smelled the fresh salt and moisture of the ocean beneath its surface. An eerie blue light filled the darkness of my prison, allowing me to see Graham crouched on the other side of the room. If he knew what was happening, I couldn't tell by the look on his face. His eyes were wide and his arms were spread open to hold himself against the wall.

The floor slid underneath the platform at my feet for another minute. I watched in awe as the room light up in a beautiful mixture of blue and white light that rippled across the walls and ceiling like a mirage. Several days in the dark had been torture on my psyche and this light aroused a new sense of hope inside me. I was beginning to feel alive again.

Once the floor stopped moving, silence filled the room. Eventually, the gentle lapping of water against the stone gave way to the stillness and I closed my eyes to savor that noise. The water was such an important part of my life. Being deprived of it for so many days had literally made me want to wither away into nothing. I inched closer to opening until Graham broke my focus.

"Do you think you should go in there?" he asked.

"Don't talk to me," I said, although wondering the exact same thing myself.

"It might be a trap." Graham sighed and then slid carefully to the edge of the opening and tested the water with his hand. He moved it back and forth a couple of times before looking up at me.

When he did, I was horrified with what I saw. "Graham," I whispered. "What did they do to you?"

His handsome face was covered in bruises and blood, and if the swelling was any indication, I think his nose was broken. The light suddenly seemed bright enough for me to notice the cuts and gashes on his forearms and hands. His skin was pale and the dark circles under his eyes probably mirrored my own.

He looked up at me with a smirk. "So now you care?" I stayed silent, refusing to acknowledge his snarky comment. Eventually he caved. "It seems as if Lucian's trust in me has run its course." Shifting so that his feet were hanging in the water, he leaned back, sucked in a breath and closed his eyes. "This feels amazing."

I was still pondering the explanation of his injuries. "Lucian did this to you?"

"Yes. Kind of." He dropped his gaze to look directly into my eyes. "You're surprised?"

"A little." I moved to the edge of the opening and hung my legs over the ledge. The warm, salty water engulfed my skin and I felt it tingle with the urge to transition. I, too, closed my eyes to briefly enjoy this sensation. I really hoped this wasn't a trick. "I thought you were his golden boy?"

Graham laughed and rubbed his hand against the back of his neck. I heard a few vertebrate pop and tried not to watch as he cracked more of his bones.

"Apparently I'm not worthy of his attentions anymore." He looked at me with a knowing smile.

"Because you tried to help me?"

"Because I tried to save you."

"Lucian wouldn't have killed me," I said with certainty, arguing that I hadn't required his help.

"He wasn't thinking clearly," Graham replied.

Just before I'd been knocked out, I remembered Lucian hurling Graham's unconscious body at me in an attempt to stop my escape. One wrong step and I could have been smashed into a boulder or pulled under the earth by Lucian's water control powers. Maybe I *had* underestimated my status as his illegitimate daughter.

"He tried to kill you," I countered with more of a question than a statement.

"Yes, he did," Graham replied solemnly.

"And that disappoints you?"

"Yes."

"Because you were loyal to him and you delivered me right into his slimy hands." My voice intensified and I got angrier with each word. Why was it that I couldn't even muster the will to want to survive until they threw Graham in here with me? Apparently my energy thrived on rage.

"I didn't deliver you," Graham pleaded. "He wasn't supposed to be there yet. I wanted to have a chance to explain everything to you and allow you to make the right decision."

"To join your cause?" I questioned with disgust. "You guys are killing innocent people!"

"People die in war, Eviana."

"You guys started this! No one wants to fight against their own kind." My stomach swirled with rage and fear and even hunger. Arguing with Graham sent life surging back into my body. "He killed my parents!"

"It had to be done."

"You killed an entire clan," I whispered, barely able to say it out loud. I had defended Graham against my closest advisors who accused him of capsizing a cruise ship. I never believed he would do something like that, until he betrayed me in Montana.

For whatever reason, Graham didn't respond. Maybe he was developing a conscience or maybe he simply knew when to shut up.

"Why did they put you in here with me?" I finally asked.

He shrugged and used the water to wipe the blood from his hands and arms. "Maybe they thought you'd finish the job for them, tart." He looked up and winked at me. I almost smiled at that thought. Almost.

"Tempting," I said, but didn't really mean it. I couldn't take someone's life. Even someone as despicable as Graham.

I twirled my feet in the water, realizing how much more energized I felt just from making contact. We needed the water to thrive. Our clans carried on as normal a human life as possible in order to blend, but without nurturing our other side, mermaids would become miserable and weak and could eventually die. Perhaps that's why I'd had no will to live.

"Did they drug you?" I asked.

"Yeah. The big guy would get me every day."

"Do you know what it is?"

"No. Why? What did it do to you?"

This time I shrugged my shoulders and noticed the aches and pains in my body. "Aside from knocking me out, I think it depressed me."

"Could being locked in here possibly have anything to do with your depression?" he commented sarcastically.

I shook my head. "It was more than that." I didn't want to tell him how every day when I felt that needle I wished my eyes would never open again.

Graham looked at me intensely for a few seconds, then found something on his arm to occupy his attention. It annoyed me that I wanted to talk to him when he'd done nothing but betray me. However, having someone share my agony with certainly made the minutes go by faster.

I watched as Graham began to flick his hand along the surface to conjure a small mountain of water before him. I'd seen him do much more than that before, so I was surprised when the underwhelming pillar of water slammed back into the pool. I was even more surprised when Graham muttered a curse.

"What's wrong?" I asked before I could stop myself.

"It seems as if that drug did more than make me sleep." He tried to control the water again several times, but eventually gave up when no more than a droplet or two would rise from the surface. "Have you tried using any of your powers?"

I shook my head. "No, I've been asleep most of the time." My talent was the compulsion, especially with humans. So keeping me knocked out while the humans tended to my needs was definitely planned. Destroying my will to live was just an added bonus for them.

"I told you he was a genius," Graham said.

"You are despicable," I spat knowing that he was admiring Lucian's manipulator skills. "Look at what he did to you. Why do you still have this God-complex for him?"

Instead of replying, Graham pulled his shirt over his head and tossed it to the side. His toned body glowed in the aquatic light, but even with the limited luminescence, I could see where he had been battered. A nasty bruise on the left side of his chest most likely meant a few broken ribs lay beneath. Despite all that, he still admired the man who'd beat him senseless.

It wasn't until Graham unzipped his pants that I snapped back into reality. "What are you doing?"

"Going for a swim."

"I thought you said it might be a trap?" I leaned forward to check if I could see anything below the surface, but the light coming from underneath essentially blocked my view. "Do you think we can get out of here?"

"Doubt it. But I need to fix this," he said pointing to his body, "so I'm going to change." And with that, he threw his pants back behind him and slipped into the water. He disappeared so fast that I didn't see him transition into his other form, although I assumed it must have been painful. The more injured we are, the harder it is.

Ever since I became a clan leader, shifting into a mermaid had become almost instantaneous. I looked down at my hip where the leadership pin was still attached to my side and wrapped my hand around it. The golden double wave pendent warmed under my touch and I felt the energy vibrating from its core. It was the first time in several days that I made contact with it, and now I wondered if that was another reason why I'd felt so lost.

The water swirled suddenly around my feet, but Graham was too quick for me to catch a glance of him. I decided that I needed to change in order to heal both physically and mentally. It was the only way for me to continue here, so I stripped off my clothes and hovered at the edge of the opening.

Without submerging completely, I willed my tail to form and gritted my teeth as the transition occurred. It was more painful than usual but at the same time it felt comforting and real. All of the aches along my body began to tingle as they healed. My vision adjusted to the darkness and I could suddenly see clearer than most animals and all humans.

With one last deep breath, I dropped beneath the surface, anxious to be in my other home.

Two

Eviana

The warm and salty water reminded me of my brief time in Florida. From the moment I was submersed, the energy coursed through my body like it was healing me from the inside out. Slowly, life began to feel right again.

Looking around, I noticed that the light came from four different directions. I swam toward one of them and it nearly blinded my vision. It was so bright and beautiful, I just wanted to be closer to it. But as I should have expected, that wasn't going to happen. My head pushed against something hard, forcing me to stop.

The perimeter of our little swimming hole was encased by fencing material. The holes were large enough for small fish to pass through, but not nearly big enough for us. Pressing my face against the mesh, I closed my eyes and let the sadness meander through me. Of course Lucian wouldn't let us escape so easily. In fact, I'm sure he wouldn't let us escape at all.

I followed the edges of the fence with my hands only to find that it extended all of the way to the sea floor. It probably dropped twenty feet below the surface and the hardened plastic-coated material was welded into the solid coral bottom. There was no way a mermaid would be able to break out of here.

Graham swam along the far edge of our underwater cage, presumably looking for a weak spot like I was. He tried to use some of his water manipulating skills to push the bottom of the fence away, but it didn't work.

Sinking to the sea floor, I curled up in a ball and tucked my head tightly against my tail. For all the energy the water initially gave to me, I felt depressed and defeated again. I could blame it on the drugs, but it really seemed as if the problem was of my doing. All of the choices I'd made over the past few months had, in a way, led up to this moment. It wasn't totally my fault, but that didn't help me feel any less responsible.

I don't know how long I was laying there feeling sorry for myself before I sensed Graham beside me. We couldn't necessarily speak underwater, but there were other ways in which we were able to communicate. Call it a natural instinct or a chemical signal, but whatever it was, we could understand each other.

I saw his concern for my well being and that made my heart beat, for just an instant. Graham was incredibly handsome and witty and he had made me question some of my relationship choices before. Our time training together at Jeremiah's made me long for his touch.

However, after his actions in Montana, I couldn't afford to allow him any further into my heart and my head.

We sat on the bottom of the ocean, surrounded by the fence and light, for what seemed like hours. In reality, it wasn't quite that long since we had to come up for air. Mermaids don't have gills, so we need to compensate for that just like the dolphins and seals.

Seals. Selkies. Brendan. How I longed for his comfort, his voice, his touch at this minute. Perhaps part of the reason why I was in such a funk was because of my ex-boyfriend. As an adult selkie, Brendan had felt the call to mate which could only be done with a human. Despite being together for eight years, his instincts took precedence and he'd left me. My pride was injured, but even more, I mourned the loss of my best friend and partner in life. For a few months we had happiness, before everything was ruined. My ability to control him combined with his instinct to have a child, didn't allow for a cohesive and healthy relationship.

When Graham and I surfaced back inside our coral-walled prison, we noticed that someone had brought us two plates of food. Without speaking to him, I pulled myself out of the water and willed my legs to come back to me. Considering our history, I might have had some concern over Graham seeing me naked, but once again, I couldn't muster up the energy to care.

"I see they've improved the food," he commented.

"Doesn't matter, I'm not eating," I said without even looking at the plates. Now that we had the light from underwater, it made it easier to move about the room and identify what Lucian's cronies were feeding us.

"No?"

"Nope," I said as I finished pulling my shirt over my head. When I turned around, I saw Graham chewing on a piece of pineapple and sifting through the rest of the items. Much to my dismay, my stomach growled. It was so loud that Graham chuckled.

"Perhaps your body wants some nourishment."

"I don't care."

"Suit yourself, tart."

I rolled my eyes and walked over to him. The smell of the food was overwhelming and I couldn't help but look down at it. "Don't call me that," I said but spoke more to the plate. There was some type of fish wrapped in a banana leaf and it smelled delicious.

"You're drooling," he teased.

"It's probably poisoned."

He bit into another piece of fruit. "Well, I haven't eaten anything solid in days, so I'll take my chances." Grabbing his plate, he sat down cross-legged on the floor and proceeded to stuff his face.

Tempted, I fought the urge to give in. I didn't really know what the purpose of my hunger strike was and how it would help get me out of here. I guess I just wanted to be difficult.

"You know," Graham started while swallowing a large chunk of food, "starving yourself will only keep you trapped in here longer."

"What are you talking about?" I groaned.

"I heard the two guards talking. The woman told the man that if you would eat something, Lucian would be much happier, which probably means you'll get out of this room."

"Really?"

"Possibly. What do you have to lose?"

"I don't want to be here at all."

"Well who does, luv?" He gestured to the four walls and his battered body, still not completely healed from his change. The injuries must have been bad. "Do you think I chose this?"

"That is exactly what you did."

"Hmm… point taken." He stood and walked closer to my corner. "I didn't actually choose to betray Lucian and suffer those consequences." His eyes sparkled when he spoke again. "I was overcome with emotion."

"Get away from me," I said. I didn't need to hear Graham profess his affection for me when it was his fault I was here in the first place.

In response, he laughed and pushed the other plate toward me. "You really need to eat."

"No."

"Your body will not be able to continue changing between forms if you starve yourself." That was a very practical argument and one that I had to ponder for a while. It felt good to transition, even if I was still trapped in an underwater cage. Plus I knew that I would have to do it again to maintain my sanity. Reluctantly, I grabbed the plate. Graham smiled and it nearly broke my composure.

I ate everything and continued to eat each meal they dropped off the next few times. Graham stayed in the prison with me and after a full day of minimal conversation, I couldn't take it anymore.

"Do you know where we are?" I asked one evening.

"Not exactly, but someplace warm and tropical." He laughed when I gave him a look. "Seriously, I don't know for sure. It seems as if the selkies speak Spanish, so I'm guessing maybe Mexico or somewhere in Central America?"

"They're selkies?"

"Couldn't you tell? I thought you had a sixth sense about them."

I leaned back against the wall and sighed. I'd always been able to recognize a selkie because I grew up with one. I never even questioned the identity of the tiny woman and the fish-smelling man that gave us our food. My mind wouldn't process anything. Suddenly, I had another realization.

"They haven't drugged me since you've been here."

Graham shrugged and began to pull off his clothes. He spoke once his shirt flew into the corner. "Maybe they think I'm addictive enough for you."

"You're a real piece of work," I groaned. I had mixed feelings about him after being trapped in here together. On one hand, I still hated him. He had lied and handed me over to Lucian. But on the other hand, I saw a side of him that I doubted anyone had ever witnessed. He was just a young guy thrown into a situation that was out of his control. It didn't mean that we were friends again, but I could sympathize a little with that kind of pressure.

Graham jumped to his feet and shimmied his pants down to his ankles. I turned my head away. "You coming?" he asked playfully.

"No, not tonight." I wanted to get in but it felt too uncomfortable right now.

"Suit yourself," he said and dove into the water without making a splash.

I spent my alone time clearing our plates and folding his clothes. It was simply something to keep me busy. When Graham finally surfaced again, I noticed that most of the bruises and cuts on his body had healed. My head also felt better, although changing forms did little to help heal the wounds on my psyche.

Depressed again, I huddled into my corner trying to will sleep to come. Being alone with my thoughts didn't help calm me down. I kept thinking about home. About Kain, Daniel, Brendan, and even Marisol. I silently cried for my parents and my uncle, realizing that I may never get to bury him properly.

Graham shuffled over to me and a few seconds later I felt his body snuggle against the back of mine. I threw an elbow in his direction. "What are you doing?"

"You look cold."

"I'm not."

"I saw you shivering." He wrapped his arm around my waist and nuzzled his head against the back of my neck. Did I admit that I was crying or let him believe that I was cold?

"I don't need you to do this," I said stiffly.

"I want to, tart," he replied and squeezed me tighter so I couldn't hit him for the *tart* comment.

"This isn't going to be a regular occurrence," I reminded him as I relished in the comfort his closeness gave right now.

"We'll see," he mumbled into the back of my head. I grabbed his arm and threw it off of me enough so I could turn and face him.

"It isn't! I still don't like you."

He smiled and snuck a quick kiss on my forehead. "I know. Now flip back over so we can spoon."

"Ugh. You are so frustrating!"

He continued to laugh as I wiggled back to my other side. Snuggling with Graham Forrester was the last thing I wanted to do, so I closed my eyes and tried to pretend he was someone else. It surprised me when the first person I thought of was Kain. Perhaps I simply worried for his well-being, since he'd been hurt the last time I saw him. Or perhaps he was the one I missed the most. Either way, I quickly found myself relaxing and was asleep before realizing what happened.

Something wet dripped on my face. I heard Graham stir beside me, but when the dripping continued, I was forced to open my eyes. Rolling over to get a better view, it took me a second to focus on the thing hovering over me.

"Ahh!" I screamed and the ratchet above me snarled, releasing another round of drool on my cheek. The dog-like creature bared his teeth at me.

"Get back you retched mutt," Graham grunted when he kicked the water sprite in the chest. It whimpered in surprise and fell back into the water.

Just as quickly, a second ratchet sprang up from the opening in the floor and latched onto Graham's pant leg. They tugged and pulled with each other until finally the door to our room swung open.

The large fish-man, or selkie as I now knew, rushed over to us and yanked Graham away from the ratchet and up to his feet. Graham struggled to find his balance and then took a swing at the man. It was easily dodged and earned the merman a toss into the far wall.

I scrambled to my knees to try and do something to fight back. Before I could even stand, both ratchets were above my head, daring me to make a move. I'd dealt with ratchets before and knew what they were capable of. Larger than a wolf and able to fight on land and in water, I understood when I was outmatched.

"What do you want?" I asked the selkie who was now picking Graham back up off the ground.

"You, stay," he grunted in my direction and I almost made a snide remark. He opened the door further and began to pull Graham out of the room.

"Where are you taking him?" I yelled. The ratchets barked at me and I instantly cowered back down. They were a little too close to my head and throat for me to challenge them. Instead, I tried to force my command onto the selkie. When he continued to shuffle out of the room, I knew that my powers had been severely weakened.

"I'll be okay, Eviana," Graham yelled back in my direction.

Without saying another word, the selkie slammed the door, leaving me alone with the two ratchets. I hunched lower to the ground hoping that they would not consider me a threat. It worked, and a few moments later I heard them slip back into the water.

I started to cry. This weakness had become a part of me that I didn't want to accept. Why couldn't I fight more? Why didn't I scream and yell and demand that they take me to Lucian? The moment I began to feel better, they took Graham away from me. I was unable to stop it from happening just like I had so little control over the rest of my life.

For hours, I stayed in that room alternating between depression and anger. I hated feeling sorry for myself yet the will to fight bled away into the stone floor. With every sob I lost another ounce of determination.

When the door opened again, I barely noticed the appearance of the ratchet's heads at the water surface. I didn't bother to look up at the person that entered my prison. Let them drag me out of here.

"Eviana?"

Lucian's voice sent shivers down my spine and that put my senses on high alert. I froze.

"I know you're awake." He pushed the door all of the way opened and for the first time in days I smelled the fresh outside air. It was filled with the scent of salt and moisture and low tide. It was lovely.

Lucian's footsteps got closer to my head. Thankfully, I had my back in his direction. "I see that you have been eating." I heard him move the empty plates to the side. "I guess Master Forrester's visit did some good after all."

I knew that he wanted a reaction from me so I tried to stay perfectly still. "Eviana, it is rude not to look at someone when they are speaking to you," he continued. "Sit up!"

My head began to pulse with a sharp stabbing pain. I remember feeling this way before and my blood boiled with rage.

"Stop it!" I yelled, unable to prevent my body from sitting upright. Lucian had control of me and it was the worst feeling in the world.

"You don't have to be so difficult, you know," he chided.

I sat up, facing my poor excuse for a father, and the headache instantly disappeared. Tempted to turn away from him, I decided to save my energy for another battle.

"Where's Graham?" I asked.

He made some sort of face before cocking a smile in my direction. "You are quite fond of him, aren't you?"

"No. I just want to know where he is." I guessed that Lucian had the ability to sense lies considering all of the other powers he possessed, and when he grinned, I knew I was right.

"It's not important," he finally answered. "I want you to come with me."

"Why?"

"Do I need a reason to request my daughter's presence at my side?"

"After keeping her locked up like a criminal? Yes, you do," I countered.

He sighed and stepped away from me. "I would like to show you to your room."

I snorted. "What? This isn't it? But it's so nice here. What could possibly top these wonderful living quarters."

"Your sarcasm is noted and it is not becoming of a leader."

"Whatever," I rolled my eyes.

"You will come with me and I will show you your room, then we will have dinner together. Am I clear?"

As if on command, the ratchets jumped up out of the water and sat down on their haunches on each side of the merman.

"You can call off the dogs, Lucian."

"Why don't you call me father."

"Why don't I call you…" The ratchets barked at me again before I could finish my sentence. It was probably for the best.

"Come," Lucian said and held out his hand. I quickly weighed the pros and cons and decided I would have a better chance of escaping once I was out of this room. I refused his hand but stood on my own and followed him out the door.

THREE

Kain

My side ached with every breath but it was still better than it felt a few days ago. Being skewered on a sword didn't bode well for me, or probably anyone for that matter. Lucian's surprise attack had nearly killed me and I would be dead if it hadn't been for the doctors. I'd also heard that Eviana kept pressure on the wound until they arrived, which inevitably stopped me from bleeding out. She had saved my life and that sent a wave of warmth through my heart.

I didn't remember too much of that night or even of the past few days. Aside from encouraging a couple of transitions in the bathtub, the doctors had kept me sedated. Every time I asked for Eviana, Julian would appear and persuade me to sleep. It felt like everyone was hiding something from me, but I hadn't been strong enough to force it out of them.

So when I awoke this morning to an empty room, I decided that I was done being a patient. A pair of sweatpants rested on the top of a dresser but I couldn't find a shirt. It was just as well, considering the entire left side of my body was still wrapped in a bandage.

Moving slowly around the room, I practiced walking without a limp. I didn't want them to know how bad I still ached. It was time for me to suck it up and resume my leadership role. Hopefully Eviana had been able to handle the aftermath of Lucian's attack without me. I instantly scolded myself for thinking that way. Of course she could handle it. She was capable of overcoming any situation. I smiled and noticed that my heartbeat sped up when I thought about her.

If I was smart, I would have given up on her years ago when it was obvious that she was in love with someone else. But I guess when you find the right person, there is nothing that they can do or say to change your mind. I'd tried to move on. I'd tried to stay away. Yet fate kept bringing us back together.

And now Brendan was gone. I should have been more ecstatic about that, but I knew how much it hurt her. Seeing her in pain broke my heart too. The best I could do right now was to simply be there for her.

And being trapped in bed for several days was not making that possible.

I opened the bedroom door and was surprised to hear a number of angry voices drifting down the hallway. Stumbling the first few steps, I was forced to use the wall as a crutch to get me closer to the kitchen where everyone was gathered. By the time I rounded the corner, I pretended that I could walk on my own and held my head high.

No one noticed me at first. I spotted Troy, the leader of the protectors, and Palmer, Eviana's cousin, throwing their arms around as they tried to convince Daniel, Marisol, and Julian of something. Two of Julian's selkies, Aleksey and Quinlan, stood to the side of the room with their arms folded across their chest. They seemed to be listening to the argument but were not offering their opinions.

The conversation suddenly ceased and everyone turned to look at me. Marisol was the first to move.

"Kain! What are you doing out of bed? The doctor said you needed bed rest for several more days!" She was Eviana's younger sister and despite the fact that I used to be her teenage crush, she also felt like my little sister as well. Since Quinlan's appearance at the house a week ago, I was no more than another patient to her.

She reached for my arm, but I pulled back at the last instant. The move sent a rush of pain roaring through my injuries. I didn't want to let it show, so I squeezed my eyes shut and willed it away. "I'm okay," I finally managed to whisper. Man, getting stabbed sucked.

"Yeah, you really look like it." That was our friend Daniel, whose sarcastic comment made me smile.

"Shut it," I groaned at him while walking over to one of the bar stools. Marisol helped me up into the chair and Daniel put a glass of fresh orange juice on the table in front of me. No one said a word.

"So..." I said. "What's going on? Where's Eviana?" I looked around the room only to find solemn and guilt-ridden faces. My heart dropped and for a second I felt dizzy.

"Kain?" Marisol laid her hands on my shoulders ever so slightly in an attempt to keep me upright. "You really shouldn't worry about things. You need to focus on getting better."

Her tone worried me. Marisol was a spoiled teen who enjoyed irritating people and fighting with her sister. This new caring and concerned Marisol only scared me into thinking the worst. "Where is she? What happened?"

When no one answered me, I tried to stand up. Perhaps my size would intimidate some of them into talking, although I wouldn't even be scared of me right now.

"Kain, sit down and relax," Troy finally said. When I settled back in the chair, he sighed and ran a hand through his hair. "Eviana's gone."

"What do you mean?" I asked fearing the absolute worst.

"Kidnapped. Lucian kidnapped her."

I jumped to my feet and ignored the searing pain. Shrugging off Marisol's hands, I began to pace around the kitchen. "How did this happen? He…he left after he stabbed me, right?"

"Yes," Troy confirmed.

"But…?"

"She went to the meeting. Alone. He got her there." Palmer's voice was shaky and weak and as her personal guard, I imagined he felt somewhat responsible.

"Why would she do such a stupid thing?" I shrieked. That girl was so stubborn and impulsive she often neglected to consider all of the consequences of her actions. This wasn't the first time she got into trouble. I looked at Palmer. "Why did you let her go?" I meant to sound more authoritative, but instead my voice cracked. I couldn't lose her.

"It wasn't my choice, man. I was unconscious!" I didn't know what types of injuries the others had endured but apparently Palmer's must have been pretty serious.

"Well, did Andre at least try to stop her?" As Eviana's uncle and second-in-command, surely he would have had more power over her. Everyone dropped their head and refused to answer me. Julian finally cleared his throat.

"No, he didn't." I looked questioningly at the selkie leader and thought I saw tears in his eyes. "He didn't stop her because he's dead. I killed him."

The words caught in my throat. Julian admitted to killing a lead member of the Dumahl clan and no one had arrested him, or punished him? Even if he was a powerful and respected selkie, he typically wouldn't get away with something like this. In a flash, it all came crashing back. I remembered being on the beach and fighting a selkie whose intentions were to simply kill me. I saw it in his eyes. Lucian had assumed control of those who'd sworn to protect us and turned them against us instead. Julian must have been under compulsion which meant that he wouldn't have been able to stop himself even if he'd wanted to. His guilt had to be killing him.

Not knowing how to respond, I sat back down and rested my face in my hands. I suddenly felt exceptionally tired and overwhelmed. So much had happened in the past few months. My father died, I became a clan leader, and we'd been fighting for our lives against Lucian Sutherland. And now, my Eviana was gone.

"We're going to get her back," Daniel said. He patted me on the shoulder. "In fact, we were discussing how to do that just before you came in." He looked up at Troy with a malevolent grin and I could tell that the two of them had been disagreeing.

"We can discuss this later," Troy said. "You really should get your rest, Master Matthew." He tried to walk away, but I cleared my throat.

"Please, Troy. I need to know how we can get her back." Either it was the desperation in my voice or the pitiful way I looked, but I saw the resolution pass over Troy's face as he pulled out a stool across from me and sat down.

"How much do you remember?" he asked and I shook my head.

"Not a lot."

"What about the meeting with Lucian?" Julian continued.

"I remember that it was in Montana and that the Council was also going to be there." Eviana and I were supposed to go together, but when I was injured she decided to leave without me or any of her sworn protectors.

"Apparently she met up with Master Forrester soon after they arrived."

"Who's they?" I interrupted.

"Caleb and Gregory," Palmer answered. "They were the only two not seriously injured in the attack and ready to fly out the next morning."

I shook my head in frustration. Eviana wouldn't even wait until her cousin was healed so that he could go with her. She was so stubborn.

"Plus, the Council's protectors were supposed to be there too," Troy added.

"What do you mean *supposed* to?" I asked.

"They hadn't arrived yet. Graham separated her from Caleb and Gregory and that's when Lucian got her."

If my injuries hadn't been so excruciating I would have torn up the kitchen. "Graham gave her to Lucian?" I yelled and Daniel's hand on my shoulder did little to diminish my rage.

"It would appear that he played some role, yes." Troy's calm and professional demeanor began to irritate me.

"So do we know exactly what happened?" I asked.

"Some of the Council's protectors found Caleb and Gregory in the forest where the kidnapping took place. Gregory was already gone, but Caleb was still alive. Lucian had used his water control to suck them both into the ground. Somehow Caleb's head remained above the surface where Gregory's didn't."

I shuttered at the thought of drowning in dirt. It was certainly not the way warriors of our kind should perish. I'd make sure we compensated their families well. "So Caleb saw what happened?"

"He saw enough. As he came into the clearing, he watched Lucian hit Eviana in the back of the head and she fell down unconscious." Troy smoothed his hair again with his hands and set his elbows on the counter. "He said that Lucian picked up both Eviana and Graham and carried them away…"

"So Graham was unconscious too?" I interrupted again.

"It would appear so."

"Huh." Maybe there was a little more to the story. Maybe a Council member wouldn't betray her like everyone assumed.

"Caleb was too busy being sucked into the earth to notice which way Lucian took them, although it wouldn't have mattered because he was trapped," Palmer finished. He seemed saddened by the loss of the protectors.

"Did you know them?" I asked.

Palmer nodded. "Caleb and I were in training together a few years ago." Our protectors were equivalent to the elite soldiers of the human military. They were specifically chosen for their athleticism and skills in fighting and swimming. Many spent a few years as a marine or navy seal before being assigned a merfolk family or individual to protect. Just a handful of powerful humans knew of their existence and would call on them for assistance with maritime defense.

"I'm sorry that we lost them," I said solemnly.

"Yeah, me too," Palmer replied.

"So that brings us to the next question," Daniel cut in. "How do we get her back?" He'd moved closer to Aleksey and I noticed that Marisol had also migrated to Quinlan's side. The tall, lanky red head couldn't hide his puppy love eyes as he looked down at her. The young selkie had been a permanent fixture by Marisol's side since his arrival a few weeks ago.

My stomach twisted in fear. What if I never saw Eviana again? I'd nearly lost her once, and I couldn't bear it if she was lost to me forever. Especially when I finally had her to myself.

"I already told you that the Council is refusing to help," Troy sighed.

"What?" I asked in astonishment. "They've turned their backs on her? After everything she's done?" My heart began to race again and I practically hyperventilated. "Where is Mr. Wallace?" Donegal Wallace was my second-in-command and I was annoyed that he had not talked to the Council yet.

"I think he's back in L.A.," Troy said. "He's been trying to work with the Council on your behalf."

"Has he asked them to help?"

"I believe so."

"And?"

"They are hesitant to do anything because the attacks have stopped since Lucian got what he wanted."

"You mean Eviana," I said.

"Yes."

"So what do you want to do about it?" I asked Troy.

"He doesn't want to do anything," Daniel spat back.

"Daniel, that's not true. We just need to decide if it's worth fighting against the Council or try and figure it out on our own," Palmer clarified.

I looked around the room and noticed that Julian seemed to have something to say. "What do you think about this?" I asked him. "Should we go after her?"

"Of course," he replied. "But we can't do it alone."

"We don't even know where she is. Lucian has allies all over the world. She could be anywhere." Troy was trying to be the voice of reason but all I could hear was him making excuses not to rescue Eviana.

"And we've already discussed a solution for that," Daniel said as he looked at me. "Abhainn."

The water sprite. He had an uncanny way of finding people in strange places. It sounded like a plan to me.

"Do you think he will do it?" I asked him.

"I'd bet my life on it. He's very loyal to her. To us," he added and waved his hand back and forth between the two of us.

"Okay. Let's try to contact him," I said.

"You may want to wait until evening," Marisol suggested. "It seems to be the only time he comes around."

"You mean he's been here and no one has talked to him yet?" I hated to be the ruling figure here, but I must say that I was a little disappointed with the lack of initiative in the group.

"He hasn't given us a chance. We've only seen fleeting glimpses of his form in the ocean and as soon as we speak, he disappears," said Palmer. "Perhaps you will have better luck."

"Perhaps."

The conversation came to a screeching halt when the doorbell chimed. "Are you expecting someone?" I asked the group. Everyone shook their heads except for the selkie leader. "Julian?"

"I told you that we couldn't do this alone. I can't risk too many, and he will do anything for her."

My stomach churned and began to fill with a mixture of anger and dread. "Who's at the door, Julian?"

Instead of answering, he walked away from us to let the guest inside. I knew who it was before I even heard him speak. But why Julian called him back here, I couldn't fathom. He'd made his choice. And he'd abandoned her.

AMBER GARR

FOUR

Kain

Daniel and Marisol gasped when Julian returned with Brendan in tow. I'd taught myself to try and be indifferent toward the guy even though he had beaten me to her. Eviana and I were always promised to each other for marriage. I'd hoped for that to happen. I was even willing to let her continue seeing Brendan. But she had picked him and instead of cutting her out of my life completely, I had to learn to compromise.

Yet when he took her to bed a few nights ago and then snuck out like a coward afterwards, I had little room left for forgiveness. She deserved someone better. Someone who would always love her like I do.

"Why is he here?" Palmer asked before I could.

Julian crossed behind us and sat back down on his stool. "I already told you. We need him."

"I don't think we do," I said without breaking eye contact with Brendan. "Besides, she wouldn't want to see him." Brendan flinched and I felt a twinge of satisfaction knowing those words bothered him.

"It doesn't matter," Julian continued. "I need him and I can't think of anyone else who would do whatever it takes to help Eviana."

I huffed at the same time Palmer, Marisol, and Daniel made a noise of dissatisfaction. Everyone in this room was willing to sacrifice something to get Eviana back. Brendan was nothing special.

He was the last person Eviana wanted to see. I was sure of it. But that wasn't the most important issue right now. We needed a plan, and whether or not it included Brendan, we needed a plan at once.

Brendan shuffled over to the table and grabbed a chair. We all watched in silence as he tossed his duffle bag to the floor and sat down without making a sound. It was comical, and perhaps rather fitting, that his chair was much lower than the rest of the bar stools. We all looked down on him like a scolded puppy. And that's exactly what he was.

Although I was the one that had been skewered with the sword, Brendan looked way worse. His dark hair hung loosely around his face and it appeared that he hadn't shaved in days. The large circles under his eyes did little to hide his distress. I wanted to tell him that he wasn't going to land an unsuspecting human female breeder with that kind of look, but decided it would be counterproductive. Still, I relished in the thought that he was suffering. He deserved it.

"Let's continue," Julian said.

Troy, in his ever-professional and military demeanor, took control of the conversation. We couldn't determine the exact logistics until we knew where she was being held. That's where I came in. I would try to contact Abhainn later tonight and ask for his assistance. The sprite was a friend of ours and I felt rather confident that he would do what he could.

"How do we handle all of the ratchets and selkies that Lucian will surely have guarding the place?" Brendan asked.

"Did somebody speak?" Daniel snapped in a very childish manner. Marisol giggled.

"You're not helping," I said, surprised that I felt kind of bad for Brendan. Well, maybe not that bad. Daniel let out a deep breath and gave me a look that said he wasn't happy.

"We will need to ask for Abhainn's assistance with that too," Julian replied.

"Well how many are going to go?" Daniel asked.

"As few as possible. It will depend on the location. We'll have to regroup once Abhainn returns to us," I said.

The doorbell rang again and everyone instantly turned to look at Julian. "What?" he asked.

"Do you have any more surprises for us?" I asked. Brendan shifted nervously in his seat and Julian shook his head.

"I'll get it," Palmer said. As he walked past us, I noticed that he was still limping. His injuries must have been pretty severe if he hadn't completely recovered yet. Troy didn't have any bandages visible, but I saw that he kept rubbing his head.

"Are you okay?" I asked him.

He looked over at me and smiled. "Yeah. It's just a headache. Remnants of my concussion I suppose."

"They couldn't break his thick skull," Daniel added with a grin. I wasn't sure how Troy would react to that comment, but when he chuckled, I understood that the two of them could joke like this one minute and argue like siblings the next. It was an interesting dynamic.

"Well, I'm glad you're here," Palmer was saying as he walked back into the kitchen with Carissa by his side.

She was arguably one of the most beautiful mermaids in the world. Her Japanese bloodline from her father's side gave her an exotic face with dark silky hair and porcelain skin whereas the height inherited from her mother allowed her to become an international runway model. She was almost a year older than me, and although I was a clan leader, I'd always felt like she was much more worldly.

She smiled at me and I couldn't help but return it. "Kain, you're moving around." In two steps, she wrapped her arms around my shoulders and kissed me on the lips. "I was so worried when Daniel called, but I was in the middle of backwoods Italy and couldn't get on a plane until yesterday."

She hadn't let go of me so I tried to shift her weight away from my side without her noticing. It didn't work.

"Oh, I'm hurting you. I'm so sorry." There were tears in her eyes and I used my right arm to reach up and wipe them away.

"It's okay. I'm glad you're here."

And I really was happy to see her. We had been kind of dating or at least toying with the idea. When Eviana left just before our wedding, Carissa was there to keep me going. Her strong personality and breathtaking beauty had me enthralled. It was a nice distraction from my infatuation with Eviana.

However, things were different now. Carissa didn't know that Brendan had broken up with Eviana because he'd felt the call. This would definitely be a game changer, but perhaps it was best to deal with one dilemma at a time.

Carissa took off her jacket and stood beside me. Her thin arm draped lightly over my shoulders allowing me to smell her wonderful floral perfume.

"Did you get a chance to talk to him?" Daniel questioned her.

"Yes." She looked around the room to include the rest of us in her answer. When her eyes landed on Brendan sitting in the tiny chair, I felt her muscles tense. She cleared her throat. "My father and my mother's clans are willing to fight with you."

I looked at Daniel and he explained. "If it comes to an ultimate showdown, we are going to need numbers. Carissa's been working the east coast."

"Well that doesn't sound very good," she smiled then continued, "but yes, my family has been using its connections to get support. I also had a chance to speak to some of the European clan leaders and they say that you have their pledges as well."

I looked at her in awe. Carissa Nakomo was going to make an excellent leader some day. I was proud of her, but it was different than my feelings for Eviana. Carissa was someone that I would work with. Someone that I'd share secrets with. A friend.

I swallowed that thought and tried to continue the conversation. "We're hoping to have some answers and more concrete plans tomorrow."

"What's going on tomorrow?" she asked me.

Instead of rehashing the last hour, Daniel gave her the six second version that ended with her in shock. "He took Eviana? Has anyone heard from her?" That last question was directed to Brendan and Daniel snorted.

"No, we haven't," Daniel answered. He moved past everyone and pushed Julian away from the refrigerator. Grabbing a few sodas, he proceeded to pass them out to those who wanted one while grilling Carissa about her latest modeling gig.

The planning session was over, and I watched as Julian and Brendan quietly left the room. I assumed that Brendan would be staying at Julian's rented house further down the beach. It was the least I could do for Eviana to make sure that he didn't stay here.

Troy was the next to excuse himself after I promised to find him if I spoke with Abhainn tonight. Carissa looked questionably at me, but I shook my head and mouthed that I'd tell her later.

Palmer whipped up some lunch for us consisting of cold cuts, sliced fruit, and chips. I was trying to stay a part of the conversations but my body was sore and tired. After an hour or so, I made my escape with the excuse that my bandages needed to be changed.

Carissa followed me to my room, dragging her suitcase behind her. It wasn't actually my house, but since Eviana and I worked so closely together, I often stayed at her place. Usually, I slept in the guesthouse above the garage. They'd moved me in here when I got hurt since it was closer to the rest of the wounded.

"Here, let me help you," Carissa said when I began unwrapping the bandages from my torso.

"It's pretty gross," I warned.

She smiled at me and I instantly felt at ease. "I can handle it."

Lifting the gauze from my skin was more painful than it should have been. Despite our enhanced healing abilities, there was only so much repair that my body could do in one day. Carissa sucked in a breath when she pulled the final bandage from my side. The wound probably resembled a gunshot injury. The sword had entered my back, just underneath my heart and penetrated all the way out through the front of my ribcage. The doctor said I had to heal from the inside out, so they hadn't closed the holes.

"Kain," Carissa whispered and I could hear the tears in her voice. "This has to end."

I wasn't entirely sure if she was referring to Lucian's attacks or my presence around the one person that seemed to be the reason for the attacks. And I didn't ask. We'd had several arguments over Eviana and I simply didn't have the energy for another one.

"So how long are you here for?" I asked then winced when she pushed the clean gauze against my back.

"Sorry," she said. "I could only clear my schedule for a week." She continued working on the wound. "Do you think this will be over soon?"

"What? Finding Eviana or getting rid of Lucian?"

She stopped wrapping the bandage and looked directly into my eyes. She was only a couple inches shorter than me, so it was easy for her to stare me down. "What do you mean about getting rid of Lucian?"

"He needs to go away. This isn't going to stop until he's gone."

"It sounds to me like it's already stopped."

I flinched and pulled the bandage out of her hand. "I'm not going to let him have Eviana." Turning away from her, I used the dresser mirror to continue my own wound care.

"Kain, that's not what I meant." I flashed her a look. "That's not *exactly* what I meant. I don't know why the two of you always think that it's your job to save the world and everybody in it. You're lucky to be alive! The last thing you need to do is go on some half-assed rescue mission." She sidled up next to me and rested her chin on my shoulder. "I'm worried about you."

I knew that she was being sincere. We had a relatively simple and honest relationship. Carissa spoke her mind and didn't hold back. There was something about it that was intriguing but there was also something preventing me from fully investing in her. I was pretty sure I knew what that reason was.

"I'm just tired," I said and tried to smile. She finished helping me with the bandages and then we climbed into bed. I needed to take a break and Carissa seemed to be jet lagged. In no time at all we fell asleep wrapped comfortably in each other's arms.

FIVE

Eviana

The moment I stepped outside of my coral prison, I fell to my knees. The bright afternoon sunlight beat down on me like a hammer, and after being trapped in darkness for so long, it was almost overwhelming.

"Oh, get off your knees. It's so unladylike." Lucian hovered over me with his arms crossed and his long blond hair whipping wildly around his head from the persistent ocean breeze. "You need to act more like my daughter and less like a victim."

"Aren't they one in the same?" I grumbled.

He leaned forward so that his face was directly in front of mine. "No. They are not." His tone was so menacing and dark, I was tempted to crawl back in the prison and live out the rest of my days in there. He must have known what I was thinking because he grabbed my arm and yanked me up to my feet. "Stop being so melodramatic."

Turning his back to me, he began to saunter down the sandy path. I noticed that we were on some type of rock outcropping and that my prison was probably just a renovated boat house since it sat along the edge of a natural canal.

Gentle waves lapped against a pristine white sand beach and the ocean itself beckoned me with its multiple shades of blues and greens. The calm seas and the occasional palm tree was the perfect picture of serenity. Too bad I couldn't enjoy it.

"Come on, hurry up," Lucian called to me. I wished that I could disappear. Following my father like an obedient dog was not my idea of a promising future.

We walked around the perimeter of the island to a rather modest vacation home. I guessed that the island itself was pretty small and assumed this was probably one of Lucian's many private estates. The home had white washed walls and was two stories high. The terracotta tiles on the roof decoratively added to its authentic charm.

"Where are we," I finally asked. Lucian saw me looking at the house and smiled.

"*Bienvenido a Mexico*, Eviana!"

"We're in Mexico?"

"*Sí.*"

"Of course we are," I groaned. Leave it to my crazy father to abduct me and flee to a foreign country. Although I guess I should be happy that we weren't in Antarctica. He probably had allies there too.

I followed him through the front entrance and past the tiny selkie women. Now that I was paying attention, I could see the trademark green in her eyes and smell that musky scent all selkies had. She didn't smile at me and I didn't thank her for holding the door.

The main floor was one large open space with a kitchen in the left corner and a large wood and tile table delineating the dining area. To the right was a set of colorful clay tiled stairs that Lucian had already climbed halfway up. His long red robe brushed ever so slightly against the steps making it look like he was floating. The effect was unnerving.

Lucian continued around the corner and down a short hallway. His figure disappeared into a room just before I reached him. I'd counted only two doors on this floor, one on each side of the hall.

"Come on, hurry along," he called from the room. I fought the urge to stop moving and see how long it would take for him to lose his patience with me. I really was beginning to feel like myself again.

I walked inside the room, surprised to see that it was quite large. The entire half of this floor made up what was to be my new sleeping quarters. Massive windows covered the far wall, providing an ample view of the ocean. Wooden shutters flanked each side and the glassless panes. They were pushed open, allowing the breeze to flow freely though the room.

On the left wall was a queen sized canopy bed complete with intricately carved wood and white mosquito netting. It was beautiful. The matching dresser and armoire reminded me of a dollhouse where everything was just a little too perfect.

There was a large dress box in the center of the bed with my father waiting patiently next to it.

"I had this made just for you," he said in a pleasant voice. When I didn't move he sighed and patted the bed. "It's not like it's going to bite you. Come here."

I checked to see if he was pushing compulsion into my mind, but lucky for him, I stayed headache free. It was quickly becoming apparent that if I played along with his charade, I might have a chance to find out more about his plans and get myself out of here. At the very least, I would get to sleep on a nice bed instead of a stone floor.

When I began to lift the lid from the box, Lucian's excitement got the best of him and he bounced on the bed. "It's from Paris. I hope you like it!" He grabbed the lid from my hands and tossed it to the side. "The silk was chosen especially for you. I know you'll look stunning in red."

I paused to glance at my doting father to see if he'd lost his mind. This sudden change in demeanor caught me off guard. Lucian Sutherland didn't have special dresses made for his daughter. He killed people.

"Go on," he said with a wave of his hands. I rolled my eyes and peeled back the pink tissue paper that had been meticulously folded around the garment inside. The first thing I noticed was the beading. Black and red crystals glistened in the light and I couldn't help but smile.

I lifted the dress, amazed with how light it was. The red silk unraveled and fell to the floor. There must have been at least five layers of red and black fabric making the skirt appear full and princess-like. The top had a fitted bodice and thin straps that crisscrossed down the back. Both were adorned with the crystal beads in a design that reminded me of ivy vines.

"So?" Lucian asked expectantly.

I was torn. The dress was beautiful but I didn't want to accept any gifts from him. At the same time, I felt like I needed to play along. I decided to go with my own question. "What's the occasion?"

He studied me for a moment before pushing up off the bed. "You will wear that for dinner tonight."

"Dinner?" I looked out the window trying to figure out what time it was.

"Yes. In one hour." He moved toward an alcove next to the window. "There is a washroom back here, so make yourself presentable. Don't be late."

With that, he swept his robe gallantly to the side and walked out of the room. In a disturbing realization, I noticed that the color of my new dress perfectly matched his red silk robe. I had a feeling that wasn't an accident.

A breeze ruffled past me and I enjoyed the smell of fresh air. I walked over to the windows and closed my eyes. Now that I hadn't been drugged for a few hours, I could see things more clearly. No one knew where I was so I could pretty much count out any type of rescue mission. It was all up to me. Lucian had something planned; it would be out of character if he didn't, so I resolved myself to discover what that was. And if it meant playing daughter for a few hours, I would do it.

I took a long shower and didn't go downstairs until the very last minute of my one hour time allotment. The dress fit perfectly, making me wonder how Lucian knew my size. I tied my hair back into a low bun so that it wouldn't hide any of the lovely details of the dress. It reminded me of something a fairy would wear, if those kinds of fairies were real. For a second I wished that I wouldn't have to burn the thing the first chance I got.

The woman selkie was waiting for me at the bottom of the stairs, her face was devoid of any type of expression even when I spoke.

"Where's Lucian?" I probably could have managed that in Spanish, but I didn't feel like being overly friendly considering she was one of my prison guards.

She understood well enough. Using her petite hands she gestured for me to follow her. I thought she would take me to the dining area, but instead we went outside and away from the indoor amenities. We were walking back toward the boat house prison and I had a moment of sheer panic wondering if this was some type of sick joke. I wouldn't put it past Lucian to give me a taste of freedom only to strip it away an hour later.

However, I let out a silent sigh of relief when we rounded the corner and had a view of the little beach. There, in the middle, sat Lucian at a small table for two sipping some type of drink. His face lit up when he saw us and my stomach twisted. I didn't want to see him so pleased.

"You look stunning as always, Mistress Dumahl." He stood and wrapped his arm across my lower back to escort me to the table. I cringed but didn't pull away. "It was so lovely outside this evening that I thought we'd have dinner with the sunset."

He turned me so that we were facing the ocean. To my right was the house and to the left, just around the corner, was the prison. I was in the middle two possibilities; adapt and stay in comfort until I planned my escape, or cause problems and get thrown back in the boat house. This wasn't a mistake on Lucian's part. He knew exactly what I'd be thinking.

Maybe I could make a run for it in the open sea. I gazed out past the small breaking waves and into the setting sun. Could I do that? I was a strong swimmer, but my water control powers were nothing to brag about and Lucian could beat them for sure. Besides, I would wager my life that he had this place surrounded.

As if on cue, which was probably quite accurate, a handful of tiny sprite heads popped up out of the water's surface and smiled at me. Their oblong heads and pointy teeth were something I would never get accustomed to seeing. Considering the mind reading ability all water fairies possessed, I tried to keep my disgust to myself.

The largest one put his fingers in his mouth and whistled loudly. On that command, at least ten ratchets jumped out of the water and up onto the beach. It was meant to frighten me, and probably also to discourage me from attempting a water escape. Instead, it angered me. The drugs were definitely wearing off now as I felt some type of emotion again. I thought of a not-so-nice way to thank the sprite in my head and smiled when he glared at me in return.

Lucian was glancing back and forth between us apparently finding our exchange amusing. He waved to someone behind me and I turned, expecting to find one of the Mexican selkies. And find them I did. All twenty of them.

"This way please," he said and gestured to the table. Only two of the selkies were carrying trays meaning this was another display of power. Lucian wanted me to know that it would be impossible to escape. Between the selkies, water sprites, and ratchets, I didn't have a chance. Although at least now I knew what I'd be up against.

"Sit." Lucian pushed me over to the chair and held it out. Such a gentleman.

"So, are you going to tell me what this is all about?" I asked while pulling the chair closer to the table before he could. I caught a slight smile on his face as he sat down across from me.

"We never had a chance to get to know each other. Your mother…"

"Don't talk about her!" I interrupted. My rage was instant and volatile. Lucian took a breath.

"All right. But I was simply going to say that I missed so much of your life and I want to know more about you."

"So you *kidnap* me? Did you ever consider a phone call or an email?"

"You being here serves many purposes," he replied cryptically. I stared at him across the table while he annoyingly unfolded his napkin and smoothed it over his lap. When he finally looked up at me I lifted my brows. "What?" he asked.

"You can't just kidnap a clan leader and expect no retaliation," I snapped.

He raised his arms and looked around. "Where are they? It's been three days and no one has come to rescue you yet."

"Why is that?" I asked, voicing something I'd been thinking about for days.

"Because I have what I want," he looked up in the air, "for now. With no more attacks, they have no reason to try and get you back."

I swallowed hard. "I don't understand."

"And here I thought you took after me," he sighed dramatically. "I have you, so they are safe. No more deaths means we both get what we want. I have my daughter and they get peace."

So the Council was going to abandon me in exchange for a cease fire from Lucian? At first it angered me beyond belief. Especially since it was one of their own who led me to my psychotic father in the first place. But then, I tried to think like a leader. If my one life saved countless others, then it would be something that I'd just have to deal with.

As though he knew where my mind was going, Lucian leaned back in his chair and smiled. "So how long does this truce last?" I finally asked.

"Long enough to bide me some time," he replied evasively. "Ah, our evening entertainment has arrived."

There was something incredibly frightening in his tone and it put me on edge. I turned in my chair to see what he was referring to and had to stop myself from jumping up and running down the beach.

"Bring him here," Lucian commanded. The water sprites and dog-like ratchets were lined up along the surf watching two very large selkies drag Graham toward us. It was hard to look at and I couldn't sit by and do nothing.

"Lucian, what are you doing?" I tried to sound reasonable but my voice was shaky.

"Young Master Forrester needs to learn a few things. Over there will do," he directed Graham's captors with a snap.

Because of the uncomfortable conversation and my interaction with the sprites, I hadn't noticed the large wood pole embedded into the beach a few feet away from us. I also didn't see the iron chain hanging from the top of it.

"What are you going to do?"

Instead of answering, he watched as his selkies locked Graham's hands to the pole. They were already shackled behind him, so when the selkie wove them through the chain, he was hanging in an awkward position. Despite this, Graham still managed to look up and give me his trademark crooked smile.

"You look wonderful, Eviana." That earned him a kick under the chin and I saw blood fly out of his mouth. I gasped in horror but Lucian didn't move. Graham spit on the ground and adjusted his position so that he was on his knees again. "Can't I even pay a lady a compliment?"

The selkie revved up to kick him again but this time Lucian cleared his throat. "Enough. Let the boy alone to wallow in his lust."

I tried to make eye contact with Graham, but Lucian shifted his chair so that I was forced to look at him. "Now, let's eat," he said.

Apparently our entertainment was over.

SIX

Eviana

Plates of lobster tails, rice, and black beans found their way quickly to our table. Lucian began to eat as though his conscious was clear, and it probably was. I had a hard time getting my stomach to settle. All I could think about was Graham, shirtless and battered, hanging up on a pole watching us enjoy this ridiculous charade of a meal.

"Eat, Eviana," Lucian said with his mouth full of lobster. I ignored him and continued to observe my surroundings. Twenty selkie guards and at least a dozen of each kind of water fairy. The selkies I could maybe control once the drugs completely wore off, but I didn't have a good defense against the water sprites. To beat them, I really needed someone like Graham on my side.

"Plotting your escape?" Lucian asked, interrupting my thoughts.

"No," I replied a little too quickly and he chuckled.

"Save yourself the trouble and relax. And eat."

"I'm not hungry."

"Eat or go back to the boat house," he replied quickly.

"What?" Was he threatening me like a child?

"If you aren't going to take advantage of my hospitality, then you can spend your days on the floor with only the comfort of your formally betrothed by your side."

There were too many things to respond to, so I went with the most intriguing. "*Formally?* You mean you don't have grand plans for the traitor and me anymore?"

I heard Graham make a noise when I called him a traitor. Good. He *was* a traitorous bastard but I also didn't want Lucian to know that his presence was bothering me. Despite our history, there was a part of me that hated to see him suffer this way.

"His future is still up in the air," Lucian replied then looked curiously at me. "Why? Are you disappointed?"

I let out a huff and shook my head. "Absolutely not. I want nothing to do with him." As if he didn't believe me, Lucian moved his chair back to the side so that I had a full view of Graham hanging from the pole. His eyes were closed and I couldn't tell if he was still conscious or not.

"Is that so?" he questioned me. I didn't answer but instead chomped down on a piece of lobster. The sweet, succulent meat melted in my mouth and it took some restraint not to gobble everything down at once. "Try this." Lucian pushed an orange colored drink in front of my face.

"What is it?"

"Just try it," he commanded again. Not wanting to be punished for this as well, I took a sip. Flavors of orange and pineapple and something else filled my mouth. The concoction definitely had a bite to it and the tartness made me cringe at first. I watched as Lucian smiled at my reaction not quite understanding what it meant.

We finished our dinner in silence. Well, aside from the occasional groan from Graham when he woke up followed by the sickening thumps of him getting kicked again. I secretly hoped that he was still getting drugged because that might help with some of his pain. At one point, a selkie pulled Graham's head back by his hair in an attempt to speak directly to him. But Graham spit in the guy's face and laughed as the selkie jumped back in disgust.

"Graham, stop!" I yelled at him, finally unable to watch any more of this. I knew that he was going to get severely punished for that action.

Lucian stayed silent and it was Graham who surprised me with his comments. "I'm okay, tart. Just playing a little mind game. Don't worry about me, ahh…" His comment was cut off by a brutal kick to the stomach. He coughed and sputtered but didn't say another word after that.

I could feel tears building in my eyes and was conflicted as to what they meant. Graham deserved to be punished for what he did to me, but I wasn't convinced this was the way to do it. Plus, Lucian was having him beat for warning me, and that meant that Graham did actually have a decent heart somewhere deep down. He may have been mislead by Lucian and his grand schemes, but Graham didn't want me to be a part of that in the end. And that is why I was bothered by his torture.

"How much longer are you going to keep this up?" I asked Lucian as nonchalantly as possible.

"Well, it appears that we're done for the evening, so we will resume the entertainment tomorrow." Without moving or voicing a command, four selkies began to remove our plates and two of them untied Graham. He wasn't fighting back and as the selkeis dragged him past me, I could hear his shallow breaths. It was then that I vowed I would try to get into the boat house tonight to check on him and his injuries.

"You and I are going to leave in three days," Lucian said suddenly, snapping me back to attention.

"Why?"

He sighed dramatically and beckoned a female selkie to his side. She began to comb through his long hair with her fingers and I watched in bewilderment as she started to braid it for him. "Why do you have to ask so many questions?" I didn't respond. "Because there are some things that need to be discussed in person."

"With who?"

"The Council."

I jumped to my feet. "Are you serious?" I was so excited. This could be my way out!

"Just calm yourself, now." Lucian looked bored and motioned for me to sit back down, but I shook my head. "They aren't going to rescue you."

"I wasn't thinking that."

"Yes, you were." He pushed the woman away and stood up to meet my eyes. "You'll see, Eviana. They are quite content with the present status quo and they won't do anything to disrupt it." He paused then said, "Or to disappoint me."

I wanted to ask him more questions. Like where were we going and how many Council members would be there. Maybe I'd get to see Adele, the American Council leader. Although she was scary and powerful, I had sensed some sort of friendship between us in the past.

But Lucian refused to answer any of my questions and speaking to his back didn't get me anywhere. I gave up by the time I followed him into the house. Exhausted and overwhelmed, I trudged up to my room. The sun had set about an hour ago yet I was surprised to see that it was only eight at night. I wanted to sneak in to see Graham but decided that I should wait until a bit later.

My head was a little fuzzy and I was beginning to feel depressed again. Immediately, I realized what happened. Instead of getting an injection, Lucian had poisoned my food or drink with that same drug. No doubt to keep my powers incapacitated despite his impressive show of security. I wanted to be angry and I wanted to scream, but right now I felt so tired I just wanted to crawl into bed.

Pushing the mosquito netting aside, I curled up on the mattress and listened to the gentle sounds of the waves lapping along the beach and the wind rustling through the palm trees. I suddenly missed my home and my friends with a vengeance. The sensation that rushed through me was so intense it took my breath away. Tears flooded my eyes. I didn't want to cry, but the last thing I remembered was the feeling of wetness on my cheeks.

I woke with a jolt. I couldn't identify what it was exactly that had pulled me from my sleep, but something had certainly startled me.

The bright moon lit my room in shades of white and blue. Shadows danced across the walls from the moving palm fronds, creating a mesmerizing scene. I looked at the clock on the dresser to see that it was three in the morning. Adrenaline surged through my body when I remembered that I wanted to see Graham tonight. Since the house was so quiet right now, I thought it'd be a good time to try and make my move.

I jumped up only to realize that I still had my fairy princess dress on. Lucian's drugs knocked me out so quickly, I didn't have a chance to take it off. Then I had another thought…what else could I wear? My eyes fell on the large, fancy dresser and armoire on the other side of the room. Hoping for the best, I tiptoed across the floor to see if Lucian had any other garments made for me.

I opened the top drawer of the dresser and nearly squealed in delight when I found underwear and socks. This was a good sign. In less than five minutes, I had stripped out of my fancy dress and changed into a pair of khaki shorts, a pink tank top, and flips flops that I found at the bottom of the armoire. Actually, the shoes were in my hand right now so that I could sneak out of the house as quietly as possible.

Getting to the stairs was easy as the tiled floor didn't creak and groan like wood did. I leaned over the railing to see if there was a guard stationed below, but saw no one. Taking it one step further, I closed my eyes and tried to use my other sense to see if I could locate anybody on the first floor. I'd only be able to detect selkies and humans, but again sensed no one.

In fact, I didn't see anyone until I rounded the corner of the beach pathway on my way to the boat house. Even then, using both sight and mind, I only counted two selkies guarding the place. Could it really be this easy? Either Graham had been drugged again or they'd beaten him so bad they didn't consider him a threat right now. That second thought made my stomach sick and I hoped he'd been injected by the big fish-man.

I watched the selkie guards from behind a shrubby bush for a while, waiting for an opportunity to make my move. It also gave me a chance to figure out exactly what my move was going to be. Brute force probably wasn't going to work, so I ruled that out right away. Sure I could fight a little, but despite all of my training with Palmer, I knew that I wouldn't be able to incapacitate two at a time.

Thinking of Palmer made me miss him, and another round of nostalgia swept through me. Although it was hard, I noticed that it wasn't quite as intense as earlier in the evening. This was good news. It meant the drugs were wearing off, which meant I could probably execute my plan.

Just as I was getting ready to walk up to the selkies my luck changed. The largest one spoke to the other then began to march down the path away from the boat house and directly toward me.

I froze, not quite sure what to do. Selkies sense of smell was akin to a dog's so I didn't think I'd go unnoticed. My heart pounded in my chest and a thousand plans scrambled through my mind.

Thankfully, I didn't have to execute any of them because the selkie abruptly turned off the path and headed straight for the water's edge.

A high pitched bark that I recognized as a selkie call carried through the night. Looking around, I waited to see who would respond. Just a few moments later, a seal broke through the surf and thrust itself up onto the beach. There was something dark and boneless hanging from its jaws that looked like a dead animal. But when the selkie still in human form walked over and grabbed the object, I knew that it was his skin.

He crouched down so that he was at eye level with the seal, and then gently removed his skin from the selkie. The two nuzzled their foreheads against each other before the human male stood and began to strip off his clothes. He wrapped himself in the pelt and dropped to the ground. After a quick shimmer and shake of his head, he had fully transformed. I'd always been jealous of Brendan's ability to change so smoothly and painlessly. Once their human skin made contact with the pelt, they became one. Selkies had a much easier transition process than mermaids, although I don't know if I'd want to have to drag a skin around with me all of the time so that I could become my other form.

The two seals frolicked around in the surf for a while before disappearing into the blackened sea. It was obvious to me that they were a couple. Perhaps they had already completed their breeding duties with the humans and could now be content with each other. Or perhaps they were just biding their time until they felt the call. It saddened me to think about their relationship and how another seemingly happy couple would be torn apart because of duty.

My heart began to ache. Even though he left me, I still missed Brendan terribly. I would probably miss him for the rest of my life, constantly wondering *what if.* I knew that I'd think about the human girl he'd have to impregnate and it ripped me apart inside. Would he still remember me? Does he feel as horrible as I do? The questions were endless but now wasn't the time for me to dwell on them.

Shaking my head to clear all of the negative emotions, I waited until the seals were long gone before completing my plan. With only one selkie guard left, I hoped that I had enough control of my powers to handle him.

"What are you doing here?" the guard asked as soon he detected my presence. I hadn't moved very far, so I knew he had sensed me just after I left my hiding spot.

"You need to sleep," I said, taking a lesson from my father. He'd tried to use his compulsion on me in Montana, and although it didn't work, giving a command to sleep was a quick and harmless way to subdue an enemy.

"I'm not tired," he replied briskly.

"You are, and you're so tired that you will sleep for an hour." I struggled to clear my mind. It was like moving through molasses. I could see the light of his consciousness, but it was dim and far away. The drugs were still in effect so I had to concentrate harder on controlling this one selkie than I had when I controlled an entire ballroom of humans.

He started to walk toward me. "You can't be here. I'm going to call Lucian and…" His eyelids began to droop.

"Sleep," I commanded and pushed through my hazy mind until I could grab his light with my sticky hand. It was how I envisioned controlling the minds of others, and after a few moments of hesitation, the selkie dropped to the sandy path and curled up into a ball. His snoring let me know I was successful and it marked my one hour countdown.

Moving quickly to the boat house, I was surprised to see that there was just a simple sliding lock on the outside of the door. Lucian must be incredibly confident with his security and his drug concoctions not to have better protection. But Lucian was also arrogant enough to assume he had the ultimate power. Either way, it only benefited my cause and with a quick push, I opened the door and stepped inside.

The lights from the caged pool below reflected throughout the room. It took a moment for my eyes to adjust but Graham spoke before I could look for him.

"Eviana?" His voice was ragged and weak. "What are you doing here?"

I turned to see him lying against the side wall. He began to push himself up but stopped when the pain apparently got too bad. "Here let me help," I said.

In the dim light, I couldn't see the all of the external injuries, but I didn't doubt their existence. I was sure that he endured more beatings once they dragged him off the beach. "Did they drug you?" I asked while maneuvering his arm over my shoulder so I could get him to the water's edge.

"Yes, I think so," he winced when I moved his legs. "You shouldn't be here."

"I know," I said.

"So why are you here, tart? Couldn't stay away from my charming good looks?" I should have elbowed him, but that would have defeated the purpose of my visit.

"Come on. You need to change." I pulled him closer to the pool before realizing something that made me blush. "You have to take your pants off."

Even in the limited light, I could see the smile growing on Graham's face. "So *that's* why you came here? You want to take advantage of me, right tart?" He started to laugh.

"Shh! Be quiet or they're going to come back."

"Don't worry, I can be quiet. It's you that might need to control your volume."

"You are such a pig." I dropped his leg to the floor with the intent of hurting him. The guy only ever thought about one thing and that wasn't very productive in situations like this.

"Ow," he said through his chuckles. "Why did you do that?"

"Take off your pants."

"Patience, Eviana. Good things come to those who wait."

"If you say one more disgusting thing, I'm leaving." I didn't really want to leave, but I tried to sound convincing. Graham started to wiggle on the floor in an attempt to remove his jeans.

"You're lying," he finally said. Crap. I kept forgetting about that little ability of his. "But that's okay. I appreciate that you came." He jerked his head to the door. "Were you able to control him?"

"Yes. But it wasn't easy. I think Lucian drugged me at dinner."

Graham kicked his left leg around like something was biting at it, so I climbed over him and pulled the rest of the pant leg off. He was able to finish the right leg himself, but paused before removing the final piece of clothing.

"You may want to avert your eyes, luv. That is, unless this is what you've been waiting for." He snapped the elastic waist band of his boxers.

I spun around with a sigh. "Can you change?" I asked the opposite wall, afraid that Graham might be sprawled out on the floor waiting for me turn around.

"Yes, I think so." I heard him slide into the water.

Walking back to the pool I knelt down and hung my head over the edge to see if I could find him. Usually the transition was smooth, but Graham was pretty injured. I worried that he might be struggling underwater.

Just a second after that thought crossed my mind, his head broke through the surface and I felt his lips brush lightly against mine. His hands gently touched my cheeks causing me to momentarily forget who was kissing me.

"Stop that!" I said and quickly sat back down before I asked for more. It wasn't Graham, per se, it was just nice to feel close to someone in this awful situation.

He laughed and slapped the water. "Come on in, tart." I put my finger over my lip in the universal sign for *shut up* hoping he take the hint. He winked and gave me an innocent look before dramatically whispering, "Are you coming in?"

I wanted to, but figured that I was running out of time. Plus, it looked like the transformation was helping him like it should. "No. But we have to get out of here."

"I agree, so what's the plan?" Graham pulled himself up onto the ledge, allowing his golden tail to dangle in the water. The fresh cuts and scrapes were healed which would be a positive sign that the internal injuries should feel better as well. His chest glistened in the reflecting light and I did my best not to stare at his merman form. I found myself remembering the night on the beach at Jeremiah's after we'd fought the ratchets when I saw all of Graham's human form. It was impressive.

What are you thinking? I chastised myself. There was something so repulsive, yet attractive about Graham that it caught me every single time. Maybe it was his power or the danger a relationship with him could deliver. Whatever it was, I needed to stop these stupid feelings and get on with business.

"Lucian is taking me to meet the Council in three days."

Graham's interest was evident. "So you're leaving?"

"I'm assuming it's only temporary, but I think you and I could break out of here permanently."

I proceeded to tell him about the selkies and water fairies that I'd observed. He agreed that I needed his help with those creatures and promised to try and avoid taking any drugs so that his powers would recover. There probably wasn't much he could do about the injections, but it was the best plan at the moment.

I told him that I'd come again tomorrow night to discuss more strategy and he seemed genuinely pleased. Before I left, he grabbed my hand and squeezed it tight.

"It was worth it," he breathed.

"What?"

"Saving you. I couldn't let you walk into a trap. I had to let you know, and even though I'm paying for it now…it was worth it."

I didn't know what to say so I didn't say anything at all. He seemed to be sincere, and it's not the first time I thought I was getting a rare glimpse into Graham Forrester's soul. There was a real person in there. Someone who could care for others and do the right thing. Someone who would have been a wonderful leader if only he had made different choices. Someone struggling like me.

I squeezed his hand back and walked out of the boat house in silence. The selkie was still sleeping nearby and thankfully his friend had not returned. There was no one there to stop me and no one to fight. I made it back to the house quickly, a little surprised at how easy this had been.

A few more days before I could get in front of the Council meant that I had to come up with an extra plan. My brain plotted and schemed all night long until I saw the sun begin to rise and finally fell asleep.

SEVEN

Kain

It was completely dark in the room by the time I woke up. Carissa and I must have slept for several hours because my mind was now foggy and weak. I tried to raise my arms overhead, temporarily forgetting about the stab wound. It still hurt but the stiffness was bothering me more. I hated to feel inadequate, and with Eviana stolen out from under us, my injury only added to the insult.

Eviana. We needed to rescue her. I needed to talk to Abhainn. Carissa's arm rested across my chest so I held it up as I slid out of bed. I felt kind of bad about sneaking off like this, but she looked content and her deep breaths told me she was still blissfully asleep.

I watched her for a few moments, stunned by her beauty. Not only was she perfect on the outside, but Carissa was a good person in her heart. She would be a wonderful girlfriend for anyone, and for some reason she wanted me. A part of me wished that I could completely close off my heart to Eviana, but that wasn't going to happen. That girl has been the most important person in my life since I was a kid. She still is. And despite knowing better, I didn't want to ruin my chances with her.

It was already night when I stepped outside on the expansive wood deck. Eviana's family had lived here for several generations, allowing them the comfort of privacy. The closest home was at least a mile away, and the direct access to the beach was a luxury for our kind. My father and I would visit this house several times a year ever since I was old enough to travel with him. Eviana and I had been promised to each other for most of that time.

I tried not to think about that part. Eviana ran away the night before our wedding and I was humiliated and disappointed to say the least. I wanted to hate her forever, but it just wasn't in me.

The nearly full moon lit up the sand in an unnatural way. Small waves echoed off the surf sending a hint of longing through me. I'd only been allowed to "swim" in the bathtub these past few days and I was itching to get in the sea. There's nothing like the exhilaration of transitioning into my other form and leaving all of the perils of the human world behind.

Looking back inside the house, I noticed only a few selkies and protectors. But more were around. Most likely hidden in locations where they could scout for trouble. Lucian had been arrogant enough to attack us at our home once, there was no doubt that he could do it again. I stuck my head back inside to tell Troy that I was going down to the beach to search for Abhainn. The water sprite had been sneaking around here, so I hoped that I'd be able to find him quickly.

The beach glowed like a moonscape and the quietness of the night calmed me. I took a deep breath to smell the air and sea, reveling in the salty yet somewhat fishy scent. It was a reminder of who we were, and now more than ever, I was craving the change. Perhaps I'd be able to find Abhainn better that way, under the water.

Instead, I decided to walk up and down the beach, taking little care to miss the surf. The sprite could use the water to move around, whether that was in the ocean or underground. I called out to him a few times, feeling idiotic for talking to myself, but I had to try. For Eviana's sake.

It had been two hours before I heard footsteps coming up behind me. They were light and graceful and almost hesitant. I turned from where I was sitting with my ocean view to see who my visitor was.

"Can I join you?" Carissa asked with a smile.

I couldn't help but return it as I patted the beach next to me. She had a flannel blanket wrapped around her and maneuvered it so that she wouldn't be sitting directly on the sand.

"Getting some fresh air?" I asked.

"Just wondering where you are." Her voice was less than confident and it worried me a little. "Have you seen him yet?"

Knowing that she was referring to Abhainn, I shook my head. "I don't know if he's really here or not."

"You're worried about her, aren't you?" Carissa said quietly.

"Of course I am. She's an important leader and practically my co-ruler. She needs to be here with her clan."

She looked at me for a moment before resting her head on my shoulder. I wrapped my arm around her back and pulled her close. "It's more than that," she whispered.

Although it wasn't a direct question, I knew what she meant. "In a way. I care what happens to Eviana, but not for the same reasons why I cared before."

Carissa didn't speak for a minute. I was just getting comfortable with the silence and the feel of her body nestled up against mine when she asked me the real question. "Do you love her?"

Did I? Yes, in a certain way. But did I love her like I wished I could love Carissa someday? "No," I finally answered.

I felt her muscles tense right before she let out a sigh. "Kain, you're lying."

"No, I'm being truthful. I swear." I turned my body to face her, wanting her to know that I meant what I was saying.

She smiled but it barely reached her eyes. "You're being truthful in your mind, but that's not what your heart is saying."

"What are you talking about?"

"I can tell when you're lying and I can tell how deep the lie goes. You are an honest man, Kain Matthew, but it's your heart that has betrayed you."

"Carissa…"

"It's okay, Kain. I think I always knew."

"Knew what?" How could she know how I felt when I didn't even really know? I've been so confused over my feelings for Eviana these past few months that it was almost a blessing for someone else to tell me how to feel.

She nudged my shoulder and then pulled away. "You've always been in love with her. Even when you were angry with her. Although I'm not sure how that's going to help you any with Brendan's return."

"Oh," I said, not knowing if I should tell her. Carissa looked at me quizzically and I decided that she deserved to know the whole truth. "Brendan and Eviana broke up. He felt the call and he can't fight it anymore." I guess that was one way to put it. Carissa didn't need to know about his return and then quick departure after spending the night with Eviana. Besides, I didn't want to think about that either.

"I see," she finally said. "Well, that does change things." My heart did something funny when I realized where this conversation was going. She turned her head and looked up at me. "Kain, I can't compete with that." Her finger pointed at my heart. "You are an amazing guy, but it's just not meant to be."

I wiped a small tear from her cheek and wished that there was something I could say to make this better. "I'm sorry."

She tried to smile again. "Don't be. But promise me that you will do this right. Don't let her miss out on the best man she will ever find." She pulled back from me again and wrapped the blanket tighter around her chest. "And you make sure that she treats you well."

I swallowed hard, not really knowing what to say. Thankfully, the moment was lost when we heard the distinct sound of galloping hooves moving rapidly toward us. Why there was a horse on the beach, baffled me for a second, until I realized what was happening.

Carissa and I stood to watch the spectacle. "Is that Abhainn?" she asked.

Sure enough, running down the beach like a Lady Godiva reincarnate was the water sprite on top of a large black kelpie. With the way the moonlight peeked out from behind the clouds, the black water horse seemed almost invisible, creating an illusion that Abhainn was flying on his own.

I remembered our ride on those magnificent water beasts when we escaped from Lucian's cave in Virginia. Carissa and I rode bareback through the night, afraid for our lives but loving the ride in the forest. She briefly grabbed my hand and I wondered if she was having the same memory. The sprite commanded the kelpie to stop just before running into us since we were too stunned to get out of his way.

In one amazingly graceful move, Abhainn dismounted and gave us a gracious nod. "Good evenin' Master Matthew. 'ave ye been waiting for me?" His Scottish accent was thick and even more difficult to understand with a neighing kelpie by our side. "Hush, Celopean. Thank ye fer helping me. Ye can go now." Abhainn slapped the horse on the rump and it immediately turned and ran toward the surf.

Carissa and I watched as the black horse trotted straight into the water and disappeared under the first wave that connected with his body. It was like he simply disintegrated into the darkened seas.

"My whole life I'd been told that they were extinct, and now I've seen them twice this year," Carissa said. She looked up at Abhainn, who had apparently fed very well because he was larger than me right now. Water sprites had a rather nontraditional diet of humans with a side of more humans. It was disturbing and I tried not to think about it. "I will leave you two alone to discuss matters."

She began to walk down the beach but I had to stop her. "Carissa, where are you going?"

"Just back to the house. Don't worry, I'm not running away yet." I could hear the pain in her voice and I hated that I was the one that put it there. I should know better than anybody how it feels to love someone who doesn't love you back. Yet even knowing that, I couldn't pretend to like Carissa when all I thought about was Eviana. It wasn't fair.

"Ye're right lad," Abhainn said, startling me.

"Huh?"

"Ye are right to let that one go when ye feel so strongly fer another." I looked at him in confusion and he tapped his head. "Mind reading. No thought is safe around me."

I cringed remembering some of the thoughts that I've had when Abhainn was around. Most were probably focused on Eviana. He laughed.

"Ye might be surprised to know that ye frequent her thoughts as well."

"I do?"

"Aye, but that is a private matter between the two of ye." He looked up at the house and I noticed that his demeanor quickly changed. "I know that she is gone."

"Lucian kidnapped her."

"Well, that is certainly a problem. Am I to guess that is why ye are waiting fer me?"

I nodded and crossed my arms over my chest. "Would you be able to find her like you found the selkies before?" I'd been there when Abhainn and his ratchet girlfriend tracked down the selkies that stole Brendan's skin.

"I 'ave already been looking. She's not in this country, that much I am sure." If she wasn't in this country, how were we ever going to find her? "Don't worry lass. I 'ave eyes and ears all over. We will find her, and when we do, I wanna go with ye."

"Of course. I wouldn't have it any other way." And I meant every word. Abhainn would be valuable in a fight and he and I worked well together. That is as long as we could find her.

"I am expecting to know her whereabouts tonight," Abhainn said as he stared off at the horizon.

"Really?" I asked, finally feeling a glimmer of hope.

"Aye."

"Abhainn!" Daniel yelled. We turned to see him running down the beach, a small flashlight beam bouncing aimlessly against the surf. "Abhainn wait!"

I heard the sprite chuckle and watched as Daniel took in his unusually large size before focusing his eyes. It was a bit unnerving how different Abhainn looked each time we encountered him.

"Hello, lad." Abhainn smiled wide enough to expose a mouthful of pointed teeth. "Where 'ave ye been hiding?"

"Hiding? What? I've been trying to talk to you for the past several nights!" Daniel glared up into Abhainn's face. "Why wouldn't you come to the house?"

Abhainn shrugged and shook his head. "Too many selkies for my taste."

I cut in before Daniel could argue more. "Why do you have that?" I asked pointing to the flashlight dangling from Daniel's hand. We could see very well at night, not to mention the moon was bright when not behind a cloud.

"I...I don't like being in the dark," Daniel said. "Plus I can use it as a weapon." I looked down at the four inch piece of metal and smiled. "I could crush your skull with this," he added as soon as he saw my reaction. I laughed. "Fine, but I could temporarily blind you."

"That is true," I conceded, and had to shield my face when Daniel tried to prove his point. "I said I believe you."

In a move so quick I hardly saw it, Abhainn reached out, grabbed the flashlight from Daniel's hand, and threw it into the ocean. "I guess ye will need to use yer natural abilities now, lad."

Daniel looked from the sea to Abhainn and back again. "Why did you do that?"

"I didn't want ye to hurt Master Matthew here and ye looked like ye were going to do some serious damage." There was no mistaking the sarcasm in Abhainn's voice and the glimmer in his eye.

Daniel huffed and threw up his arms. "Very funny, Abhainn." He moved into the sprite's personal space. "I think I saw a water bottle over there. Maybe you'd like to spend some time thinking about how you don't have to be so rude?"

There was a hint of stiffness to Abhainn's shoulders. Daniel's water control was probably good enough to capture the sprite if he took him by surprise. For a moment I wondered if he was serious, but when I saw Daniel wink, I knew he would never do that to our friend.

"So do you know where she is?" Daniel asked, moving a few steps away and getting to the real reason why he was here.

"Not yet," Abhainn said.

"But we should know soon," I added before Daniel could say anything else.

"Aye, I think..." Abhainn's words were suddenly cut off by the soulful howl of a hound. Shivers ran down my spine, recognizing what that sound meant. I looked at Daniel who was frozen in place, and then to Abhainn. His face lit up as we all turned to face the water. "I think we will know now."

In an instant, Abhainn's body exploded into millions of water droplets and fell quietly into the surf. Daniel and I backed up, trying not to get any on us. "'I really hate it when he does that," I said.

"Is he okay?" Daniel asked. I looked out into the glimmering sea and saw the sprite's head emerge next to the ratchet that was calling for him.

"Yeah," I said. "I'll bet that's Isabel."

"That ratchet?"

"Yes. I think she's Abhainn's girlfriend." Eviana and I had a chance encounter with the two of them in a nearby park. Apparently we'd interrupted a private moment leading me to believe they had a romantic relationship. "She's the one who found Brendan's attackers."

"Interesting," Daniel said quietly while watching the two water fairies converse in their human forms. "I hope she found Eviana."

"Me too." I sighed, trying to relive some of the tension in my neck. The movement sent a wave of pain through my side and I cringed. I was tired of being in pain.

"You should sit down," Daniel said.

"I'm fine."

"You're not. You were skewered. By a sword." He stepped in front of me. "Stop trying to pretend it doesn't hurt."

"I'm not."

He huffed. "I don't get that macho thing you all do. Why can't you just admit when you need help?"

"I'm fine," I said a little louder.

"Whatever. Be in pain." I had to smile. Daniel couldn't be mad at anyone. He was simply too nice and nurturing. "Here he comes."

I turned to see Abhainn walking out of the surf and marveled as he shifted himself into clothes. I was slightly envious of their abilities to turn into anything or anyone. Although, I'd rather protect humans than eat them, so I suppose I was better suited as a merman.

"Well?" Daniel eagerly asked.

"Did Isabel know anything?" I added.

Abhainn smiled and slapped both of his hands on our shoulders. My body protested, but it was a secondary concern. We waited for him to say something. Finally he spoke.

"We found her."

EIGHT

Eviana

Due to my late night escapade, it was almost noon before I opened my eyes. My plan was in place, along with a backup. Now, I just had to find Lucian and swallow my pride.

It wasn't hard. Well, the finding Lucian part anyway. My pride was another story. Making my way downstairs, I noticed the dining room table overflowing with fresh fruit, breads, and juices. It was a spread fit for a queen. Or king.

Lucian sat on end of the table adorned in his trademark red and black. Only this time, he wore a pair of red parachute pants made for the beach and a short sleeve black silk shirt that hung open to display as much skin as possible. My appetite disappeared instantly and I frantically wished I had another backup plan.

"She wakes," Lucian cooed. He stood to greet me but I diverted my path to avoid his touch. Then I remembered that I needed to play along.

"Good morning," I said. "What's the occasion?"

Lucian watched me skirt around his presence and I could see a hint of disappointment cross his face. Masking his reaction, he smiled obnoxiously wide. "Why, this is all for you. Our first breakfast together. Or, more like brunch at this late hour."

There was something knowing in his tone. My heart pounded and my breath caught, worried that he found out about my late night visit with Graham. Picking up a piece of pineapple to avoid his stare, I shrugged. "What can I say? It's the fresh air."

"And how do you like your new accommodations?"

"It's okay," I said nonchalantly.

He laughed and moved back to his seat. "I imagine it is. Please, sit down. Our main course is almost ready."

I reached the heavy wooden chair but the women selkie pulled it out for me before I had a chance to refuse. Putting on my best sarcastic smile, I nodded my head and accepted the favor. If her snort was any indication, she knew that we were just playing nice.

"What's the main course?" I asked, stuffing another piece of fruit into my mouth. It was simply too delicious to refuse.

"Ceviche and truths," Lucian replied then chuckled when he saw my face. "I think it's time that you and I got to know each other better. Ask me anything you want."

I thought about that for a moment before shaking my head. "Nope, I think I'm just fine living in blissful ignorance."

"Why must you behave that way? You are a clan leader now, not a spoiled brat."

I tried to stay calm but it was taking a lot for me to remain seated. "I've already learned everything I want to know about you," I managed to say through gritted teeth.

"You know what they want you to know." Lucian waved his hand around and took a long sip of his drink. "I'll bet Marguerite never mentioned me, did she?"

My heart ached and tears blurred my vision the second he mentioned my mother's name. I stayed silent. Not because I didn't have anything to say, but because I couldn't force the sound past my clenched throat.

"She was something else." He stared out the window with a look of someone who deeply admired my mother. It was an expression he didn't deserve to wear.

"Then why did you murder her?" I asked, seething with emotion.

"You know the answer to that already," he replied without looking at me.

I was ready to argue but a loud crash by the front door interrupted our conversation. Someone yelped in pain just before the sound of rattling chains echoed through the room. Two large selkies dragged Graham across the threshold and into the dining area. Lucian smiled in a way that chilled me to the core, especially when he turned to watch my reaction.

Graham's arms were pulled tightly behind his back, exposing his chest under the unbuttoned shirt. His hair pointed in all directions and his right eye was red and swollen. Bruises still covered his body, leading me to believe they were fresh from this morning since he should have recovered a little with his change last night. Why did they continue to beat him?

"Ah, another meal for you and another chance to torment me, I suspect," Graham said with sarcasm all the more defined by his accent. "Isn't this swell."

The selkie on his left pushed him forward and Graham tried to fall to his knees. Although the position of his arms wouldn't allow him to reach the ground, his body weight was enough to pull his guards off balance. I watched with amusement as the three of them toppled to the floor. He certainly didn't make their job any easier and I knew that this was why Graham was still being abused. It would probably stop if he would be a good little prisoner like me.

I tried to relay that through my eyes with no luck. Graham wasn't looking at me, but Lucian was. His face twisted with delight. Without missing a beat, Lucian stood and pulled out a chair in the center of the table. Once Graham was sitting, Lucian motioned to the guards who promptly removed the chains from around Graham's arms.

He massaged his wrists and smiled up at the selkies. "Well, it's been fun mates. I must say that I usually enjoy that kind of treatment but with faces much prettier than yours."

The largest selkie slapped him on the back of the head in reply. Graham laughed then winced when his neck snapped forward a little too hard. It was almost as if he enjoyed being in pain.

"Why is he here?" I asked Lucian, afraid that I would have to witness another beating while trying to eat.

Graham, with his mouth full of bread, looked up at me with sad eyes. "I missed you too, tart."

Lucian chuckled and motioned the selkie woman back into the room. She set a plate in front of each of us and began dishing out something from a large bowl. When she got to me, she made no attempt to hide her annoyance as she slammed the large spoon against my plate, splashing ceviche juice and octopi tentacles everywhere.

"He's here because we all need to talk about the future," Lucian stated. Graham coughed loud enough for me to know it wasn't an accident.

"You mean the one where I die in your retched little prison?" He still had a mouthful of food, making it hard to understand him.

Lucian took another sip of his drink and smacked his lips together. "No, Master Forrester. I mean the one where you marry my daughter and help lead the revolution." This time I was the one who nearly choked.

"I will not marry him," I replied at the same time Graham said, "Excellent!"

"I'm afraid that you have no choice in the matter, daughter. It has been arranged for a long time."

I stood up fast enough to knock the chair over. "I don't care and you should know that I won't marry someone just because I'm told to do so."

"She does have a point," Graham added before shoving a bite of ceviche in his mouth. I glared at him but Lucian distracted my response.

"You don't understand, Eviana. You and Graham were always supposed to be together. It's in your blood."

"What are you talking about?" I yelled, aware that the selkie woman was trying to reset my chair, but not giving her any room to do so.

Graham stopped chewing long enough to look at Lucian. "Our bloodlines?" The way he spoke led me to believe he knew something about this already. Sitting back in his chair, Graham smiled. "That explains a lot."

"Will somebody please tell me what you're talking about?" I grabbed the chair from the woman's grasp and dared her to challenge me. After a few seconds, she threw up her hands and stomped away, muttering something in Spanish.

"Please sit down," Lucian said calmly.

"I'd rather stand."

"It's okay, tart. You can tell him the truth now," Graham added.

"What are *you* talking about?" I asked, taking a step in Graham's direction, still holding the chair. Perhaps it could serve as my weapon.

"The fact that you have and always will be attracted to me," he said, tipping his glass.

"I am not attracted to you."

"Liar."

"Enough!" Lucian interrupted and slammed his hand against the table. "Eviana, please put the chair down and have a seat so I can explain."

"Or you can sit right here," Graham said while patting his lap.

"Or I can smash this over your head," I sneered and lifted the chair slightly. It was always so intense around Graham. Every feeling I had seemed exaggerated when he was nearby.

Graham stood abruptly and raised his arms out to the side, inviting an attack. "Oh, how I've missed our sparring sessions, tart."

His smile made my heart skip a beat and I scolded myself for that. Letting Lucian's words finally sink in, I turned toward my estranged father and ignored the beautiful man in front of me. "Why do you think that he and I are supposed to be together?"

Without saying a word, Lucian motioned for me to sit again, so I reluctantly pulled my chair back to the opposite side of the table. Perhaps there really was an explanation as to why I've felt so fiercely attracted to Graham, even after he betrayed me.

"Have you ever heard of genetic compatibility?" Lucian asked me.

"Maybe," I said, trying to search my brain for a reminder.

"It's basic mate selection. Those with compatible genes tend to seek each other out."

"Like I said, I'm irresistible," Graham joked and I threw an orange at him. He laughed while proceeding to gorge himself with the pastries.

Lucian sighed and continued. "This process seems to be especially prevalent in merfolk. Particularly now that there aren't as many of us left in the world." He paused long enough for me to realize I was holding my breath. "However, there are some bloodlines where that selection has waned and others where it has intensified over the centuries."

"Why is that?" I asked, suddenly interested in this history lesson.

"To preserve our powers." He stood and walked gracefully over to Graham. Placing his hands on his shoulders, Lucian leaned forward close enough to whisper in Graham's ear. "There aren't very many of us left so our bloodlines subconsciously choose each other."

I was confused. "You and Graham have the same blood?" And he wanted me to marry him? "Wouldn't that make us siblings?"

Lucian and Graham both laughed. "Oh no, that is definitely not the case. But just like your mother and I, Graham is genetically predisposed to be your mate."

"My mother loved my father very much," I said through my tight throat.

"I'm sure she did. But just like you love that selkie and Master Matthew, your blood is still attracted to Graham."

"I don't love them," I whispered, barely able to emit any sound. Why should I love Brendan? He was gone and I would never see him again. And Kain. My stomach twisted in pain thinking about him. Was he even still alive? I couldn't bear it if he died. Did that mean I loved him?

Graham cleared his throat, forcing me to focus on him. "Realize something, have we?"

"My mother loved my father," I repeated instead of addressing the thoughts racing through my mind.

"She did," Lucian confirmed. "But she couldn't stay away from me either. Hence, you," he said and nodded in my direction.

I chose not to acknowledge that comment. I couldn't stomach the thought of my mother spending any personal time with Lucian. Learning that she had lied to me my entire life was disappointing and heartbreaking enough. How had my father handled it all so well? His strength and willingness to raise me as his own created a whole new sense of respect for him and I suddenly felt sick with sadness.

"Are you okay?" Graham asked, drawing my attention back to him.

"She's fine," Lucian answered for me.

"Perhaps you could feel some sympathy for her. This can't be easy to hear," Graham replied in my defense.

In an instant, the two selkie guards came back into the room and yanked Graham out of the chair. He tried to reach for his drink but it was slapped out of his hand before he could take a sip. Graham struggled against them, at one point seeming to almost break free. The largest selkie smiled a second before he slammed his head into Graham's face. Graham yelled out in pain and his nose began to bleed profusely.

"Stop!" I called out to them. "Why are you doing this, Lucian?"

My father stood with his arms crossed and a tense look on his face. A long moment passed before he looked up at me. "I'm making a point."

Now on his knees, Graham tried to tilt his head back to stop the bleeding, but the selkies held him tight. He coughed several times before Lucian continued.

"He may be your natural mate, but he still needs to learn his place in this world."

"And you are the only who can teach me, right?" Graham asked with a huff. Lucian flicked his hand and the woman selkie marched over to him. Without saying a word to her master, she turned and walked straight toward Graham. The surprise on his face was evident until she reached forward with unexpected speed and punched him three times in the stomach. He doubled over in pain, his arms pulled taut in the opposite direction.

"Lucian!" I yelled.

The selkie left the room in a daze. Lucian's control over them was astounding. If I had all that power, I could get us out of here. Trying to push a command into the selkie's minds, I searched for my little room and their lights. The haze still clouded my head but I used all of my concentration until a spiteful laugh broke my focus.

"You're going to break a blood vessel in your head, daughter. The compulsion needs some work." Lucian made his way to the table and grabbed an apple. Tossing it up and down, he paced around the room while the selkies moved Graham closer to the door.

"He needs to learn his place, and you need to learn how to use all of your gifts."

"I think we both know our place," I whispered, not quite knowing how to respond. I was afraid to ask what he meant about my gifts.

"You both have immense power," Lucian continued. "So much power, that there are many who would not be pleased with this union." The sharp sound of his teeth biting into the apple made me wince.

"We don't know what you're talking about," I said.

"No?" Lucian asked but looked at Graham. Turning toward him myself, I expected Graham to back me up. He didn't say anything.

"Graham?"

"Eviana...I...," but before he could finish one of the selkies punched him in the face hard enough to knock him out. My stomach plummeted. Graham was not my most favorite person in the world, but he didn't need to be treated like this. Plus, he was about to tell me something.

The shuffling of feet accompanied the tears burning in my eyes. The guards pulled Graham out the door and presumably back to the boathouse. I promised myself that I would check in on him again tonight. It was a long walk between here and the prison, and I knew all too well what the selkies could do to Graham in that amount of time.

Lucian cleared his throat. "Now that the distraction is gone, I'd like to pick up where we left off."

"What do you mean, Lucian?" I couldn't hide the weariness in my voice.

He took a final bite of his apple and then threw it out the window opening. Making another grand performance out of moving to his seat, he put his feet up on the table and crossed his arms behind his head.

"I'm going to tell you all of the secrets your mother kept hidden during the last seventeen years."

My instincts were telling me to run. I knew what was coming next would change everything. Did I really want to learn anything else? My old life seemed like it didn't exist anymore. Like none of it was ever true.

But then I thought about my friends back home. Many of them were injured or worse, so perhaps leaving that part behind would help me get through the next two days. At least until I could get in front of the Council.

Letting curiosity get the best of me, I sat down in the chair next to Lucian's and prepared for the worst.

NINE

Eviana

"How much do you know about your mother?" Lucian asked. Thinking the question was obnoxious and insensitive, I glared at him. "Eviana?"

"What do you mean?" My mother came from a powerful family, and had she wanted the notoriety, she probably could have held a seat on the Council. I knew that she was strong and formidable, and that her clan respected her immensely. She was a loving mother, a caring sister, and a good wife. Or at least that's what I wanted to believe.

"Let me rephrase," Lucian continued. "Do you know why we are at war?"

"Because of The Legacy." It was a term used to describe merfolk's ability to control humans and other water creatures. Those that wanted to practice their birthright didn't care to live amicably amongst the humans anymore. They wanted to rule the world and all living creatures in it like we had done in the past.

"Yes, The Legacy. But do you know why it's important now?"

I rolled my eyes. "Just get on with it, Lucian."

He smiled and patted the top of my hand. I pulled away as quick as I could. "Patience, daughter. You may be surprised at how many of us want to declare our rightful place in society. In fact, clan leaders and Council members throughout the world have been doing just that in times of need."

"How?"

"Inciting wars, ending conflicts, controlling natural disasters. Humans always find a way to explain it with science and religion. But what we've really been doing over the past century or two is grooming them for what is to come." Taking a moment to pause, he sipped his drink. "Allowing The Legacy to thrive would actually make things a lot easier for them."

"For who? Humans?"

He nodded and smiled. "Yes. Remove all choice and you have peace."

"And robots," I added. Did he really believe this? "So, what? A few powerful Council members and clan leaders decide what is best for the entire world?"

"Exactly," he replied with amusement.

Shaking my head, I continued asking questions. "And you're hoping to be one of them?"

"I *am* one of them," he said. "As was your grandfather, Graham's parents, and a couple of the Council members you know and many you have yet to meet."

"My grandfather? Who? Papa Dumahl?" It was common practice in leadership families to maintain the surname, even after marriage.

"The one and only. He worked on this for most of his life." My mother's father was a supporter of The Legacy? I needed a moment for that to sink in. "We almost had your mother convinced to join our cause, until she met Charles," Lucian scoffed. "He wanted to blend in with humans and raise a family in his little peaceful bubble. What a waste of talent."

"Excuse me?"

"Your mother." He smiled at me again in a way that made my skin crawl. "Her power was amazing, but she refused to use it to further our cause. Did you ever see her water control?"

I was overwhelmed. Once again it seemed as though everyone in my life was a liar. My mother told me that she'd endured an arranged marriage and she also never showed us her water control. That was something I didn't even know existed until I met Abhainn. Seeing my face, Lucian sighed.

"I guess she didn't want you to know about that either," he said quietly, and I almost believed that he felt something. Be it pity or disappointment, I didn't care.

"So how are you involved in all of this? Are you the...leader?" I asked, trying to find another word.

He laughed and reached for another apple. "Am I the leader? Not quite. But I am important."

"A touch of humility never hurt anyone," I added sarcastically.

"Why be humble when I am stronger than most merfolk in the world?" His arrogance was astounding. But I picked up on one of the words.

"Most?" For once, I smiled. "Oh, say it isn't so. There are a few more powerful than you?" I feigned a shocked look complete with a hand over my heart. The corner of Lucian's lip curled up and instantly worried me.

"Yes. There are a few. But I'm convinced I can bring them over to the dark side." I didn't appreciate his attempt at humor. Just as I was getting ready to ask for more information, the woman selkie shuffled into the room with a distressed look on her face.

"What is it?" Lucian asked.

"A phone call. For you. Urgent," she replied in broken English. Narrowing my eyes at her, I wondered how often she pretended not to understand the language. She caught my stare and smirked. I wished my compulsion was working better.

Lucian stood but I grabbed his arm to stop him. "What have you done to my powers?" I didn't really want to ask him, but I needed to figure out how to get out of here.

"What are you talking about, daughter?" he asked with fake concern.

"Why have you been giving me drugs to dull them?"

His laugh echoed through the room as he removed my hand from his arm. "Oh, my dear. We have so much to discuss. Those drugs are not meant to dull your powers, but to set you free."

And with that, he walked out of the room, leaving me in a state of confusion. Free me? I had no idea what he was talking about. As if on cue, my vision blurred slightly and my head began to spin. He did it again. Every time I ate or drank something here I was drugged.

Even though I'd only been awake for a couple of hours, my body wavered with exhaustion. Not knowing what else I could do at this time, I decided to go back to my bedroom to lie down. Trudging up the stairs, I tried to process all that Lucian had divulged. My family line was connected to Graham's somehow. And all of those related to us seemed to be the ones causing this civil war.

My mother's petite frame and beautiful face came to the forefront of my mind. I still missed her terribly, even though my emotions were torn. She lied to us all. About my father, her powers, and her connections to this war. Ever since I assumed leadership, I realized how unprepared I had been for this responsibility. We never talked about my powers or the real reason why she was so against practicing The Legacy. Her personal connection to those fighting with their own species had been unknown to most of us. Evidently, she decided to leave that part of her behind and make a life with my father instead. My sister and I were raised in a home with two loving parents who did their best to hide the true nature of our world from us.

As I began to drift off, I thought about how furious she had been when I left with Brendan. She was angry enough to shun me from my clan. I now realized how much her disappointment with my behavior must have been difficult for her to manage. As a clan leader, and an apparently very powerful one at that, she must have looked like a failure to her peers. How could she direct her people if she couldn't even control her own daughter? There was probably little else she could do at the time. She needed to prove her strength to her people.

At some point, my thoughts shifted into dreams. I was swimming with my father off the coast of a tiny rock island near our home. It had been my eighth birthday and I'd requested a picnic in the water. Since my sister and I hadn't been old enough to transition yet, a picnic in the water meant playing in the waves and pretending we had a tail. My father tied our legs together with a ribbon, while my mom laughed and set up the blanket.

He dove into the first wave and disappeared beneath the ocean. My sister and I shuffled after him, wanting so very much to swim as freely as our parents. We jumped and squealed as waves crashed into our legs and halted our chase. My father broke through the surface, flipping backward and beckoning us to catch him. Almost at once, the water wrapped itself around our waists and carried us out to sea. I kicked my legs back and forth as if they had transformed into a tail and laughed when I saw my father squirting water out of his mouth like a fountain.

Without really trying, my sister and I twirled in circles and moved around each other with ease. I caught sight of my mother on the beach with her arms spread wide, turning round and round in a solo dance. The sound of her laughter carried across the sea and soon my sister and I joined her in celebration. We were floating through the water like true mermaids; exactly what I wanted for my special day.

I sat up in bed with a jolt. The dream was actually a memory, pushed deep into the back of my mind. I'd lied when I told Lucian that my mother never showed us her powers. She had manipulated the water to move us through it like dolls. And that wasn't the only time she played with my sister and I that way. Whenever I begged to go swimming with her, I realized she was using a little bit of her powers to keep me by her side. Like a mother dolphin with her calf, she let us believe we were doing it on our own, all the while fiercely protecting us by her side.

As I wiped away the tear falling down my cheek, there was a knock at the door. I had fallen asleep on top of my bed, fully clothed and completely drugged. The fading blue in the sky gave way to brilliant oranges and pinks, letting me know that I slept through the entire day. I really needed to speak with Lucian more about the drugs and their effects. I was tired of wasting time.

There was another knock, only this time is was louder and more urgent. Rolling out of bed, I opened the door, not really caring who saw me in my disheveled state. The woman selkie looked up at me and shoved a wooden tray into my hands.

"Dinner," she said in English before turning and walking away. She moved quickly, almost as if she were afraid to say anything more.

I looked down at the tray that held a covered plate, a glass of water, and a vase with a single flower in it. My stomach turned at the sight of the black orchid, remembering the last time I received one of them. Apparently it was Lucian's favorite flower; a sign that he expected complete cooperation from me.

Moving further into my room, I kicked the door shut and threw the orchid on the ground. I didn't want it staring at me while I ate. Although looking down at the plate, I wondered if I should risk being drugged again at all. No doubt there was something in the water or the food, and if I was going to see Graham again tonight, I needed to have all of my strength to get past his guards.

I lifted the plate off of the tray and discovered an envelope underneath. The red wax seal with the letter "S" embedded in the center once again reminded me of a note Lucian sent to my home. He'd warned me that others would suffer for my choices, and they had. Many had died, many were still healing. My hands shook with sorrow and regret. Again, I thought about Kain, my sister, and my cousin, Palmer. I even thought about my Uncle Andre and Jeremiah Williams who had both paid the ultimate price for my decision not to join Lucian in his war. So many people had suffered because of my actions. How many more would I send to a similar fate?

The single piece of paper held the familiar writing of the man who has caused so much pain in my life. I read it with clenched teeth.

Dearest daughter-

I regret that I must miss our dinner tonight as business takes me away for a few hours. Please enjoy your meal while you think about what we discussed earlier today. Tomorrow I will explain more, and answer the questions you may have. We will also prepare to meet with the Council. Proper attire will arrive for you in the morning. Sleep well.

Lucian

I tossed the note next to the orchid on the floor. Proper attire? It was like I was his personal doll to dress up and parade around for everyone to see. I was tired of this charade. Yes, there were still many questions left unanswered, but I would survive without knowing the truth if I could just get out of this place, right?

Two more nights and I could leave here forever. I had a rough plan that involved the Council meeting and creating some type of distraction so that I could try and plead my case. The Council wouldn't ignore my request to take me away from him. They couldn't. I was the Dumahl Clan leader. I needed to be with my people. Surely they would understand that.

And if they wouldn't listen to me, I had another option. Graham. He was a Council member. I just had to convince him to help me in this matter and we should both benefit. I could go home and he could…well, he could do whatever he wanted to do. After the beatings and abuse he sustained at Lucian's hand, I hoped that he would be finished with the charade and see Lucian for what he really was. Deadly.

With newfound energy and excitement, I anxiously awaited for the sun to set so that I could sneak into the boat house again. After five minutes, I realized that I could pass some of the time by taking a bath. A nice long soak in the tub always did wonders for my nerves.

Pulling on the terrycloth robe that appeared in my bedroom today, I began to fill the tub with a perfect mixture of cold and hot water. The water heated up rather quickly and in no time at all, the bathroom was filled with steam.

I wanted to brush my hair, so wiping the fog away from the mirror I looked at my reflection for a moment. I swear I saw wrinkles around my eyes and gray circles underneath. Did I always look so haggard and old? Was this what was to become of me?

"Aye, only if ye stay in this place."

My scream escaped before I could stop it. I spun around fast enough to throw my hairbrush at the water sprite now standing in the bathtub. It passed clear through him and slammed against the far wall. He smiled and looked at me quickly before turning away like he was shy. I realized a little too late that my robe had loosened and now exposed much more skin than I wanted him to see.

"Abhainn! You scared me half to death," I scolded him while trying to hide my blush and tie my robe. "What are you doing here?"

"Ye might wanna keep yer voice down, lassie. We don't want the dogs to hear ye."

"Well, maybe next time you can knock." I looked at his aqueous body and shook my head. "Or at least give me some warning."

He grinned. "I didn't wait until ye were already in the tub."

I sighed then smiled. Before I could stop myself, I flung my arms around the sprite and nearly dragged him out of the water. "I am so happy to see you."

He reached up and pulled at something in what I assumed would have been his jacket pocket. I felt his body shudder just before a white handkerchief appeared in his hand. He dabbed at the tears moistening my eyes. "I am happy to see ye too, Mistress Dumahl. Ye 'ave worried us all."

"How did you find me?" I asked, taking a step backward and pulling my hair out of my face.

"I 'ave my ways," he said with a wink and I had to grin. Abhainn did have his ways and they always seemed to work.

"Is anyone else with you?"

He shook his head and looked around the room. "No. Not yet. But they are close."

"Who is?"

"Yer rescue team, my lady." My rescue team? I found myself immediately thinking about Kain. Did he come for me too? But before I could ask, Abhainn cut off my thoughts. "I must go now. Too many eyes and ears."

"Abhainn, no! Wait! You can't leave me here."

He smiled at me with his mouthful of pointy teeth. "I am not going anywhere, lassie. Just be patient and try to stay calm."

"But who..." I started to ask until he tipped his hat to me and exploded into a million tiny water droplets. I watched as they gathered themselves and rushed up the faucet back the way I assumed he got into the building in the first place.

I fell back onto the toilet, my legs shaking and my heart pounding in my chest. Maybe I wouldn't need my plans after all. Maybe Abhainn and the rest of my rescue team could get me out of here for good. I needed to tell Graham right away.

But I didn't move. Did I want to leave this place? Yes. Did I want to learn more about my mother and her powers and how I fit into this story? Absolutely. One path would send me home yet have me looking over my shoulder every waking minute. The other option required me to stay until I learned what I needed to so that I could end this once and for all.

I didn't know what to do, and once again I feared that I would make the wrong choice.

TEN

Kain

"Why does it have to be Mexico?" Daniel whined.

"What's wrong with Mexico?" I asked, curious as to why this would be an issue for him. It wasn't like he was going on the rescue mission.

"Too many bad memories," Daniel said and shook his head. He physically shuttered as he looked off in the distance, remembering something I didn't want to know about. "Is he sure that she's there?"

"Abhainn is good at this. He left this morning to check it out for himself." I expected to get word any time now on whether or not he'd located Eviana. Isabel had enough information from other ratchets and sprites who were apparently loyal to her. They reported a gathering of water creatures around a tiny island off the tip of the Yucatan Peninsula. It sounded like the perfect hideout for Lucian and an even better place to hold a clan leader captive.

"I still want to go with you," Daniel said while handing me a knife.

I was in the process of packing the weapons bag although I hoped that it wouldn't come to actually having to use them. "I know, but..." I winced when I reached a little too far. I really needed to get in the water and heal. It had been long enough.

"But what? You're injured. Palmer still has a concussion, and who wants to trust the selkies after what happened?"

"They were under Lucian's control," I reminded him.

"Exactly. What's stopping them from losing it again? If he catches you guys, you will never get out of there alive."

He was right. I knew with the utmost certainty that we had one chance of getting Eviana. If we were caught, we were dead. I tried to hide my fear. It wasn't that I was afraid of dying for her. I was more afraid of what Lucian would do to her in retaliation. Or to our people.

"That's a risk I'm willing to take. Besides, I need you to stay here and look after Marisol."

Daniel rolled his eyes and slumped down into a chair near the kitchen table. I continued packing until the silence got the best of him. "Fine."

"Fine, what?" I asked.

"Fine. I will stay here and babysit while you go and play knight in shining armor." He crossed his arms and sighed dramatically. I had to laugh.

"You're doing the right thing," I said.

"Yeah, whatever."

I finished packing up the duffle bag full of knifes, hand grenades, and a couple of Japanese short swords. It was Julian's weapon of choice, but I preferred to stick with my natural abilities. I'd been practicing my compulsion and my water control seemed to improve every day. It was like a switch had been turned on and I suddenly knew exactly how to manipulate the element with very little effort. The compulsion I would save for a few choice selkies if needed.

As if listening to my internal thoughts, Brendan appeared on the beachside deck and knocked on the door frame. Neither of us acknowledged his presence, so he walked inside and sat down next to Daniel.

"I need to talk to Marisol," Daniel said and quickly jumped out of his chair then disappeared around the corner. I would thank him for that later.

"Do you need any help?" Brendan asked.

"Nope."

After a full minute of silence, he spoke again. "Abhainn will find her, right?"

I stopped filling the snack bag I was working on and took a deep breath. Do I respond or do I stay silent? I decided to listen to my heart. "Do you really care?"

As though I stabbed a sword through him too, Brendan recoiled in shock. "Of course I care! I love her more than anything in this world!"

"If you truly did love her, you would have left a long time ago." My voice wavered with anger and a thousand other emotions.

Apparently we were going to have this discussion and I wasn't fully prepared to filter my words.

Brendan jumped to his feet and leaned across the table toward me. "You would have loved that, wouldn't you? Having her to yourself. Going through with a marriage she never wanted. It would have been perfect for you if I would have stayed in Washington, right?"

"Yes," I said through gritted teeth. "She would have had a chance to choose me."

"She always had that chance. I never stopped her." He moved around the edge of the table so that we were looking at each other eye to eye. I could see the lines around his face and the grey tone of his skin. He looked like hell and I smiled. "What's so funny?" he snapped.

Ignoring his question, I stared into his eyes. "She doesn't want you now."

He sucked in air then turned away from me. "But I need to help her."

"No, you don't. We have this under control."

"Lucian will have an army of selkies. You need us. Plus, I have to do this." His tone softened and I almost felt bad for him. Almost.

"She won't want to see you," I said, confident in my words.

He sighed. "I fear that you may be right. But I can't live with myself for hurting her. I need to make amends."

I had to laugh. "Make amends for using her and then leaving her? You have some nerve." I moved back toward the table and finished shoving protein bars and trail mix into the bag with a little too much force. "For the life of me, I never knew what was so special about you." I probably should have stayed quiet, but at this moment I didn't really care.

"You can't help who you love," Brendan whispered.

"True. But you can control the way you treat them," I spat back. Did he really expect me to understand what he did?

"I can't help the way I feel. It's like there's something pulling me away from her, but yet there is a part of me that can't let go." He walked back to me and sat at the table. I stopped packing and looked down at him. Taking a deep breath, I tried to rein in my anger.

"I've heard others talk about the call. They say it's unlike anything they've felt before. Like nothing else matters except for finding a mate."

Brendan laughed, but it wasn't pleasant. "Yeah, nothing like having an outside force steer you toward the first female who shows the slightest bit of interest in you. Or not. Sometimes I find myself wanting to be near married ladies or older women, like my seal has a mind of its own when it's seeking a mate. I think I spend more time fighting the call than anything else." He leaned forward and rubbed his hands over his head.

I was uncomfortable this entire conversation, but I needed to know more. "Have you succumbed?"

Brendan's head snapped up and he looked angry. "What? Are you asking me if I impregnated some unsuspecting human?" I didn't reply and he glared at me. "No! No, I couldn't do that to her!"

"Who? Eviana?"

"Yes, Eviana you ass! I told you I still love her and I wouldn't do anything to hurt her."

"But you left," I said. "After you spent the night with her." I couldn't help but let the venom slide into my words. Not only did the thought of the two of them together make me angry, but seeing her so upset the next day solidified how much I disliked the selkie. I always have and I probably always will.

Brendan had the decency to look ashamed. "I never want to be with anyone else."

I knew that this moment was a turning point for us. The subject was uncomfortable, the emotions were raw. He didn't need to tell me all of this, and yet, here he was having a conversation I'm sure he dreaded just as much as me. Thankfully, we were saved.

"Have you heard from him yet?" Troy asked and sauntered into the kitchen, conveniently blocking my view of the selkie. I watched as Brendan looked up at our lead protector and then out the window. Our conversation was officially over and hopefully we wouldn't have to speak this much ever again.

"Not yet. But I'm ready." I gestured toward the bags on the table and watched as Troy dug through each one. If it weren't for his military background, I may have been offended. Troy like to triple check every preparation. It was one of the qualities that made him so valuable.

I grabbed a glass from the cabinet and turned on the faucet. Nothing came out. Lifting the handle up and down a few times, I glanced at Troy and was just about to ask him if the water had been turned off when I heard a noise. It sounded like a muffled curse. I looked back at the faucet and watched as a tiny sprite dropped into my glass.

"Abhainn?" I asked, holding the glass up to the light to get a better look.

"Put me down," he said softly in his tiny form. I set the glass in the sink and Abhainn grew a few more inches. By the time he stepped over the edge of the glass, he stood about a foot high and stared at me from the kitchen sink with his hands on his hips.

"See something ye like, lad?" he asked with a slight attitude.

"Good to see you too," I said, trying to lighten the mood. Apparently Abhainn didn't like being smaller than the rest of us.

He looked past me toward Brendan. "Ah, the selkie returns again. So how long are ye going to stay fer this time?"

Brendan huffed and walked over to stand behind Troy. I saw Abhainn crack a smile.

"So did you find her?" I asked.

"Aye, she is there." I let out the breath I'd been holding and looked at Troy. He, too, seemed relieved. I didn't care what Brendan felt. "But it's not going to be easy. I had to hide amongst a school of fish to get away from that compound."

"Compound?" Troy asked.

"Aye, he has the whole island to himself. That alone is not bad, but it's the hordes of ratchets and selkies guarding the place that'll be the problem."

"I told you," Brendan said and it took every part of my control not to punch him.

"Is he coming with us?" Abhainn asked.

"Unfortunately," I replied and Troy snickered. It was probably immature, but I didn't really care anymore. We had a mission to accomplish. "So how do we get there?"

"Ye will need to fly into Cancun and we can boat from there. But once we get within a few miles, I think our best strategy is to go in underwater."

"Do we have enough help?" Troy asked.

"Aye, I believe so if we take him," he nodded in Brendan's direction, "and Isabel. She may be able to acquire some of the ratchets and he can serve as bait."

Brendan rolled his eyes while I thought about him being torn apart by the other selkies. A tiny part of me felt ashamed for enjoying that vision, so I pushed it down and out of the way. "I can use the water to help capture the sprites and Troy, Julian, and Brendan can take care of the selkies."

Abhainn winced. "Be careful which sprites ye control there, lad. Wouldn't want ye accidentally drownin' me."

"I won't. I've been practicing." I felt like a first year student, needing to prove myself to Abhainn who had taught us so much.

"I know. Just giving ye a hard time." He leaned out to look around me and at Brendan. "And I know that ye won't screw up."

"What?"

Abhainn tapped his head. "Mind reading. It's a lovely thing." Brendan returned to his seat at the table and didn't say another word. My guess was that he didn't want Abhainn reading any more of his thoughts.

"So when do we go?" I asked.

Abhainn shook his head and began to climb out of the sink. "I need an hour. But ye can get on the plane now if ye want."

"An hour? Why?" Troy asked, but I feared I already knew the answer to that.

"I just travelled thousands of miles underground. I need to eat." Abhainn fell to the floor and grumbled another curse that I fortunately couldn't understand through his thick accent.

"Are you feeding here?" I thought about all of the humans nearby and then about one selkie in close proximity.

Abhainn's laughed filled the room despite his tiny size. "No, lad. I will not eat one of those ghastly dogs." He looked up at Brendan. "Even though that would solve quite a number of problems."

"Very funny," Brendan said, but I saw him glance nervously at the deadly sprite.

"Please be discrete," I begged. It wouldn't be prudent to have humans disappearing right now.

"Always am," he replied with a mouthful of intimidating teeth. Pushing past me, he walked toward the front of the house and looked expectantly at Troy. Getting the hint, Troy stepped over him and opened the door just wide enough for the sprite to fit through. He tipped a tiny aqueous hat in my direction and then dove off the front porch and disappeared into the ground. It was the closest source of water and he'd used the underground system to move around Eviana's property before.

I didn't know who he was going to eat, and I did my best not to think too much about it. We needed Abhainn at his full strength, so

I refused to let my personal feelings interfere with what needed to be done.

And speaking of personal feelings, Julian had joined Brendan at the table by the time I turned around. I hadn't even heard the other selkie come into the kitchen. Julian wasn't one of my favorite people at the moment, considering he'd asked Brendan to come back here. He knew this and addressed his comment to Troy.

"I have a jet waiting at the airport. It's at our disposal whenever you are ready." Where did Julian get a jet? The selkie sure did have a lot of friends who seemed to always do him favors.

"We leave in fifteen minutes," Troy said and then turned to me. "Please collect all of the bags while I get Palmer. He's not totally recovered, but he wouldn't be happy if I made him stay here."

"I'm taking Malcolm as well," Julian cut in and Troy stiffened. Malcolm had been the one to injure Troy during Lucian's attack on the house. He nearly killed him, and although he was under Lucian's compulsion, it no doubt bothered Troy.

I thought about my own aches and pains and wished that I had a little more time to try to transition. It would be important once we arrived, and since I hadn't been in the ocean for several days, I worried about how much the change might take out of me. But it was too late now.

With a nod in my direction, Troy left with Julian and Brendan following closely behind. They spoke quietly to each other, no doubt discussing strategy and war tactics. As much as I despised the two of them right now, I was somewhat glad that they would be there fighting on our side. The selkies can be ruthless, and with Julian's guidance, Brendan and Malcolm had become impressive fighters.

I grabbed the bags from the table and headed toward the front door. A laugh from upstairs caught my attention, so I stopped to listen. The voices were mumbled, but I could tell that they were having a good time. I picked up Daniel, Carissa, and Marisol's voice as they joked and teased with each other.

Do I say goodbye? What if this was the last time I would see them? Then I scolded myself. If I thought like that, than I would surely die. I had too many responsibilities here along with too many friends counting on me to lose this battle. Plus I had a clan to lead.

It still surprised me how much I thought about my leadership and how it had changed me. My people came first. They had to. So was I doing the right thing? In my eyes, Eviana came before them. Perhaps it was wrong, but she had always consumed most of my heart. We ruled together, therefore we needed to fight for each other. She would do it for me. I owed it to her.

Without saying a word to my friends, I walked outside and climbed into the SUV. Just a few moments later Julian, Brendan, Malcolm, Troy, and Palmer joined me. No one spoke. It was an uncomfortable silence that lasted the entire way to the airport and nearly the whole length of the flight. Troy and I discussed the attack plan a few times, but most of my thoughts were tied up thinking about her.

I wanted to tell her that I was coming and all she had to do was hang on a little longer. I wanted to tell her how much I missed her voice and her laugh and her face. I wanted to tell her how much I loved her.

ELEVEN

Kain

We waited until dusk before setting sail to the far outer reef that housed Lucian's island. Abhainn had procured a modest motor boat and as we splashed through the surf, I wondered if it was even necessary.

"We need to save our strength," he said, reading my thoughts once again. "Lucian has at least a dozen selkies and even more ratchets patrolling the sea. This is not going to be an easy task."

"Brendan, Malcolm, and I can handle the selkies," Julian said.

"No, ye will need his help," Abhainn replied pointing to me. "Can ye control them long enough fer these dogs to finish the deed?"

I smiled when Brendan snorted. "Yes, I can. But it must be done quickly so that I can trap some of the ratchets too."

"Aye, although we are hoping that Isabel can persuade most of them to look the other way."

"She can do that?" Troy asked.

Abhainn's face lit up with such admiration, I felt like we were intruding into a private moment. "She can do many things."

He drove us through a series of swells that drowned out any remaining conversation. I sat in the back of the boat, careful not to fall into the water. Abhainn steered the thing like a new driver which made me wonder if he'd ever been behind any type of wheel before. I saw his shoulders shake in laughter at my silent question.

Brendan sat on the bow of the boat, speaking to Julian. My blood still boiled from our earlier conversation making me regret bringing him along. It was my job to help Eviana, not his. What if she wanted him back after this? What if they tried to be together again? After my conversation with Carissa, I realized just how much I was willing to sacrifice for Eviana. Even someone as beautiful as Carissa paled in comparison to what I felt for the one who'd been promised to me for nearly a lifetime. I don't know if I could deal with Brendan swooping in and stealing her from me again.

The boat engine suddenly cut off and we were thrust into an eerie silence. The slapping of the waves soon subsided and the stillness of the night felt like the calm before the proverbial storm. I lifted my head to the now darkened skies and marveled at the millions of stars glittering back down at us. They seemed so peaceful and content; a promise I hoped one day I would be able to know again.

No one spoke as Abhainn twirled his now human-sized hand in the water. He hung his head over the side of the boat like he was trying to see through the shadowy surface. His face was calm while he hummed a hypnotic tune. We all remained silent as we watched this strange behavior.

A splash in the distance made me jump and I noticed the rest of the group straighten up in alert. Only Abhainn seemed at ease. He continued humming another round of the chorus until a large canine-like creature darted out of the water by his hand. Abhainn whispered some words to the ratchet and patted its head slowly.

By sheer instinct, I jumped up in preparation for a fight. Julian snarled and Troy pulled a knife from somewhere on his body. The ratchet growled and Abhainn shot us a warning glare before whispering again to the sprite. Without taking its eyes off Troy, it shook its head until long, auburn tendrils of hair appeared around a beautiful, perfectly symmetrical human face. Two slender arms wrapped around Abhainn's neck and with one quick movement, he lifted her into the boat. All of the men instantly dropped their gaze to avoid staring at the striking naked female who seemed more than comfortable in this form.

"Hello Isabel," I said and extended my hand. She hesitated a moment before grasping my arm. She pulled me so close to her that I could smell the sea on her neck. Her face perused my cheek as she inhaled a long breath. It was a very intimate position and I had to force myself to remain calm.

"I remember you. You are zhat love sick merman, *non?*" she asked with a thick French accent just before pushing me away. Taking another deep breath, she quickly jerked her head toward the front of the boat and looked at Brendan. "*Oui*, and I remember zee smell of you, dog." Brendan looked at me in confusion.

"Isabel is the one who found your attackers," I explained.

"Oh," he said then also extended a hand to the naked ratchet. "Then I owe you my life. Thank you for helping me. For…for helping us all," he stuttered. Isabel's beauty and danger were enough to make any man forget how to speak. I suspected it was one of the qualities Abhainn most admired.

"Aye, lad," he said and the two sprites smiled knowingly at each other. "My love, what have ye discovered?" Isabel glanced around the boat, clearly deciding whether or not to disclose all that she knew. "It's all right. Ye can trust them. They are my friends."

She nodded and then sighed. "He had promised zhem a place by his side in zee war, but I persuaded zhem to reconsider. I zink zhat most will follow my orders. But zere may be a few zhat will need to be incapacitated."

"Are you certain of this?" Troy asked.

She turned so quickly that spittle flew from her mouth which had just transformed into one full of sharp teeth and a few large canines. "Oui! Zhey vill listen to *moi*! I am zee queen!"

"Queen?" I asked Abhainn and he nodded.

"Aye, Isabel is a leader herself. She comes from very powerful family, and most ratchets will listen to her." He smiled down at his love and squeezed her tight. "Ye 'ave done very well."

She lifted her head up to kiss him and for the next few moments we had to sit there while Abhainn expressed how grateful he truly was.

Finally, Troy cleared his throat. "We should go."

Isabel growled again but Abhainn laughed. "Aye, lad. We shall." He pulled away from Isabel and looked at each of us. "Follow closely behind and once we get there, stick to the plan. In and out without Lucian noticing. That is what we want."

Isabel stood and stretched, much to the discomfort of the rest of us on the boat. It was hard enough not to notice her beauty, but her standing there in perfect form forced us to concentrate on the preparations. The selkies each pulled out their skins from the bags and wrapped their clothes in a watertight duffle. Malcolm changed first. The minute he wrapped his pelt around his back like a blanket, he dropped to the floor of the boat and shimmered just a brief second before fully becoming his seal. I remember Eviana telling me how graceful their transitions were, but to see one myself was truly magical. I envied their ability.

Julian tied the small bag of clothes around Malcolm's neck and gestured for him to go into the water. Their transitioning power was maybe worth my jealousy, but the seals struggled to move well on land. Malcolm undulated and grunted until he finally had enough of his body weight over the edge of the boat to slide in the water the rest of the way.

Brendan was next, followed by Julian. Abhainn and Isabel grabbed hands as they dove over the side. I watched the five of them gather together several feet away from the boat. The seals twirled around and dipped their heads above and below the surface. Abhainn and Isabel stole another moment to kiss. Everyone seemed content. It was as though we weren't heading out into trouble.

"You ready for this?" Palmer asked, shaking me from my thoughts. I nodded. "She'll be fine." He slapped his hand on my shoulder, which sent several waves of pain through my body. I tried not to grimace. "We'll get her."

"I know we will," I smiled back at him. Troy helped steady Palmer as he removed his shirt. It wasn't until then that I realized how serious Palmer's injuries must have been. He still didn't have all of his strength back and I feared that the damage to his head may be more permanent than anticipated. He probably shouldn't be here, but I kept my opinion to myself.

Palmer and Troy jumped in the water together and remained underneath just long enough to make me worry. Transitioning when injured is not a pleasant experience. When they surfaced, I could see the pain in Palmer's eyes yet he kicked his tail and stretched his muscles to settle into his new form. Troy gave me the signal that they were okay, so I passed him the bag of weapons. He strapped it around his waist then pulled them both under the boat to join the other awaiting selkies and sprites.

Now it was my turn. Stripping off the last bit of clothes, I looked up into the sky. It was time to get my Eviana back. I sucked in a deep, shuddering breath and fell into the sea head first.

Letting gravity pull me under as deep as she dared, my other nature began to take over. At first it was spectacular. The feel of the salt water made my skin tingle and the muffled sound of the moving currents set my mind at ease.

And then the pain hit me. My ribcage burned from the inside out as my lungs began to expand and push against the partially healed hole in my chest. A particularly gruesome spasm sent my back into an arch and I screamed at the searing pain. In all my life, I've never experienced a transition so hard. I could feel every bone reforming, every wound healing. It was as if this were my first time. I should have demanded they let me practice at Eviana's before coming here. Now I would be weak from dealing with the change. I would be a liability for the team.

In the last few minutes, my vision cleared enough to see Troy and Palmer waiting and watching under the boat. It was slightly embarrassing that they may have witnessed my struggle, but when another round of throbbing pain pulsated through my body, I didn't care. Eventually, the soreness turned into a prickly sensation and I watched as the last of my stab wound closed itself and disappeared forever. My scales suddenly reflected the limited light from the night sky and the breath I'd been holding no longer felt forced. The transition was over.

I turned toward Troy and gave him a thumbs up. His slight nod indicated what the tension in his body couldn't hide. He had been worried for me. For us both. And now we'd proven that we could handle this.

I followed them to the others and surfaced just long enough to grab a lungful of air. We still had several miles to swim, but no one wasted any time. For ten minutes, we all swam at a fast pace in the darkness only breaking formation when we had to surface. Isabel changed into a form that reminded me of a dog mixed with an eel, and the ease at which she moved through the water caused a bit of jealously to stir inside of me. Not too long ago I was ready to attack her kind, and now I marveled at their uniqueness. We had always been taught that water sprites were extinct. And now here we were, working side by side to help each other. These past few months have really been eye opening for me in so many ways.

Abhainn stayed in his human-like shape but his legs had almost disappeared in a stream of bubbles. It was like he simply fused with the water and each molecule moved in sync wherever he passed. He wasn't using his arms or kicking his legs, he simply glided effortlessly and gracefully through the landscape.

Isabel suddenly stopped and we almost swam right past her. She effortlessly switched into her human form and put both arms up telling us to stay put. We gathered together behind Abhainn who watched her intensely. She swam ahead of us in a surprisingly human way, looking all around her as if she were waiting for something.

In an instant, I saw them. Their canine heads and eel bodies slowly surrounded Isabel. Abhainn jerked forward, but I grabbed his shoulder without thinking about it. Isabel didn't want us to go with her for a reason, and when Abhainn nodded at my thoughts, I let go and retreated behind him again.

One of the ratchets shimmered and then turned into an odd shape, more akin to a troll than a human. His hair fell down a back that was full of lumps and muscles where they shouldn't be. The pronounced jaw and enlarged forehead only added to the image of a creature from another world.

He hovered in the water as Isabel swam closer to him and extended her arm. He grabbed a hold of it with both of his then kissed the top of her hand. She smiled and he gestured to those around him. Without opening their mouths or making a sound, they had a conversation. At last, the troll man pulled away from her and swam in the direction of our boat. There were at least a dozen ratchets following behind, but not a single one of them looked at us as they passed.

Isabel came back to us and motioned toward the surface. Without hesitation, we kicked our way up to the top so we could speak to each other. Or at least the sprites and the mermen could, the selkies had limited communication skills in their seal form.

"Zhey say that she iz at zee boat house. She goes zhere every night to visit zee boy."

"What boy?" I asked, even though Isabel was clearly speaking to Abhainn.

"Graham Forrester," Abhainn replied. "Lucian has been torturing him in an attempt to persuade Eviana to join his cause."

Brendan snorted the same time I asked, "How do you know this?"

"Isabel and I collected information." And as though that were the end of the conversation, he quickly changed the subject. "Those ratchets will watch over the boat and surrounding waters, but it looked like only half of them listened to Isabel."

"Zhose ignorant *féerie*," she spat. "I vill personally see to it zhat zhey are punished for zhis."

"Ye have us all to help, my love," Abhainn tried to calm her. "I will enter the boat house first through the water, while the rest of ye watch my back. If ye can subdue enough of the selkies, we will need to get her out of the house and onto the shore as quickly as possible."

We all nodded in agreement and dove beneath the surface once again. In no time at all, we could see the faint outline of the rocky coral island. And just as quickly, the first attack occurred.

With a speed I didn't know possible, two large selkies darted between us and cut off Julian, Malcolm, and Brendan from the rest of the group. I spun around just in time to see Julian go after the smaller one while Malcolm and Brendan fought against the larger seal. Their teeth were bared and even under the water I could hear the shrieks and cries each time a fang pierced through skin. Julian was handling himself, but the selkies were evenly matched.

Red water seeped from the chaos like a drifting fog. Troy and I started to go after them, but Abhainn held us back and shook his head. He pointed to the island and motioned for us to follow. We had agreed to let the selkies battle each other; our skills would be better served on other fronts.

And no sooner had that thought crossed my mind, did I see a wall of teeth moving in our direction. A wail from the selkie battle nearly made me lose my concentration, but then I saw Isabel rush toward the ratchets with nothing but fury in her eyes. She doubled in size by the time she reached the first sprite and ripped into its neck. The others, momentarily stunned by her brutality, watched in fear as she tore through three ratchets in a matter of seconds.

Then as if something jolted them back to life, they screamed and darted toward Isabel and the rest of us. Without a second thought, I threw up my hand and stopped the four that were coming at me with an invisible liquid barrier. I trapped them within my walls and watched with a smile on my face as they moved like they were stuck in molasses.

A trail of bubble wash sliced through my barrier in an instant, and when it came out the other side, all four ratchets were reduced to nothing but bite-sized pieces. Abhainn wiped his mouth and winked at me before swimming over to Isabel to help her finish off the rest of the sprites.

Troy yelled just in time for me to dodge out of the way of a selkie attack from below. Using my water control, I spun the selkie around faster and faster until he landed on Palmer's knife. The blow didn't kill him, but he sank to the bottom and slithered away into the dark. By this time, our selkies rejoined the group, bloodied and battered. Brendan had a huge chunk of skin missing around the side of his face and Malcolm was nursing a bad flipper.

Abhainn whistled and motioned for us to keep moving forward. There were no more attacking ratchets and selkies for a while, which seemed to worry us all. Where did they go? What were they planning? Surely we didn't defeat every last one of them.

When we reached the crashing waves delineating the shallow surf of the island, Abhainn signaled for most of us to move onto the beach while he and Isabel made their way to the boat house. The six of us used the surf to glide onto the sandy area and quickly changed. Of course it was much easier for the selkies, but my transition didn't hurt nearly as bad, and in no time at all I was walking on two legs again.

Troy took over command at this point and had the selkies patrol the beach while we made our way to the boat house on foot. I hoped this was the right decision, since the selkies were relatively incapable of dealing with water sprites. Hopefully Isabel had persuaded more of her kind than she knew.

I was thankful for the darker evening and lack of moonlight. Crouching down into a slow jog, we followed Troy along the path that Abhainn said led to the boat house. In the distance, I could see the lights from the main building and I wished that Eviana wasn't in there. We only had one shot at this, and if we picked the wrong house, all would be lost.

Shaking my head to get rid of those negative thoughts, I focused on the path in front of us. Something shifted in the scrubby bush beside us and we all froze. The soft mumbling sounded like a person, and they seemed to be closest to me. I signaled to Troy that I was going to take a look, and with his nod, I stepped off the path to find the source of the noise.

It took just a few steps before I found the selkie curled up on his side and fully asleep. He was in human form, but the gun on the side of his hip indicated that he was most likely a guard. Why would one of the guards be sleeping on the job?

Palmer snapped his fingers and when I looked up, he pointed to another patch of bushes further up the path. I crept over next to Palmer to see yet another selkie, fully decked out in guard weapons, sound asleep and slightly covered by a loose piece of brush.

"What is going on?" Palmer whispered.

"I'm not sure, but it's certainly not hurting our mission. Let's keep going," I said.

Three more sleeping selkies later, we'd reached the boat house. Every one of the shifters appeared to be in a deep sleep and just before opening the door I realized what must have happened and smiled. Eviana.

"It's her," I said in awe.

"What?" Troy whispered.

"It's Eviana. She's the one that put them to sleep with her compulsion. Instead of killing them, she made them sleepy. It's brilliant."

"Go, Eviana," Palmer cheered. And then we heard the scream.

"Was that her?" Troy asked.

Before I had time to answer, my body jumped into motion and I threw my shoulder into the large door of the boat house. That was her scream, I would know it anywhere.

The room was dark inside except for a slight glow emerging from the water where Abhainn now hovered, looking rather satisfied with himself. He smiled and gestured in my direction.

I followed his gaze until I saw her. My heart stopped when her face lit up. No one could compare. I knew that now more than ever. Her eyes shimmered with unshed tears, and she pushed something off her lap so she could stand. I realized belatedly that it was another merman, but it didn't really matter.

As she ran toward me with outstretched arms, I knew that I would never let her go again. This time she would stay with me forever.

Twelve

Eviana

"Kain," I breathed. I forced my arms around his chest and squeezed for fear that this was all a mirage. In the few days since my capture, I'd constantly wondered if he was alive. Not only had he survived, but he was here to rescue me. I sobbed uncontrollably as he rubbed his hands over my back.

"Shh, it's okay, Eviana. I'm here now and I won't let anything happen to you."

His voice, his smell, his touch. Why had I not realized how much all of them meant to me before now? Kain in my arms felt right. Felt safe. Without giving it a second thought, I reached up and grabbed his face. Pulling it toward mine, I kissed him. Hard. It was as if a gate had been opened and there was no controlling the flood of emotions gushing through my body. I'd missed him so much. I wanted him so much. He was mine.

Kain kissed me back with just us much passion, surprising us both. His soft lips and gentle touch contradicted the urgency erupting inside. My heart pounded in my ears as the world faded around me. It was just the two of us in this moment.

When he pulled away, I felt a sudden pang of despair. It was like I couldn't get enough of him. Was it because of the situation and my fear that I'd lost him? Or was it that I'd finally recognized what I wanted? I tightened my hold on him and nestled in against his chest. It wasn't until then that I realized he was completely naked.

But he didn't seem to mind as he continued to hold me close. "Are you hurt? I heard you scream," he finally asked, breathless from our kiss.

"I'm okay. Abhainn just scared me." I looked up into his eyes and smiled. "You're alive."

He laughed and kissed my forehead. "Yes, I'm alive and now I'm rescuing you."

"Thank you," I whispered just as a shadow appeared in the doorway. In an instant, my fluttering insides shriveled and died when I recognized the person standing there.

Still wrapped in Kain's embrace, I had a moment of sheer confusion. My heart skipped, but not in the way it used to. The time alone had allowed me to grieve for the loss of my selkie and I'd prepared myself to never see him again. And now, he was in Mexico.

Without thinking, I asked Kain, "What is he doing here?"

Brendan moved further into the room and I found myself pulling away from Kain to stand closer to Graham and Abhainn. "Eviana, I'm here to help." He reached for me, but I flinched. I couldn't let him touch me. Not now. Everything was so jumbled inside. Seeing Brendan had opened the hole in my heart that barely had a chance to heal. I'd ignored that hole when I saw Kain, but now it was fresh and raw.

"I already have help," I said with a shaky voice. "I don't need you."

"Evs, please..."

"No. Don't. You can't call me that anymore." I could feel the tears in my eyes and the lump growing in my throat. I didn't want to have this conversation.

"Well, as much as I'm enjoying this soap opera, perhaps we can get out of here ? What do you say, tart?" I had forgotten about Graham and his words snapped me back into action. I looked at Abhainn.

"Can we escape?"

"Aye, but we 'ave to hurry."

"Can we take him?" I asked, nodding to Graham.

Abhainn sighed. "Do we have to?"

I looked closely at Graham. The fresh bruises and gash on his forehead were signs that he'd been beaten again. If I left him here, Lucian would surely kill him. I couldn't have that on my consciousness.

He led you to Lucian. My inner voice was right, but during the past few days, I saw how that plan had backfired for Graham. He was just as much a victim as I was. It wasn't right to leave him here to suffer.

"Yes, we have to. We can figure out what to do with him later," I replied. Kain and Abhainn exchanged a look. I purposely didn't glance in Brendan's direction.

"Fine," Abhainn said. "But we have to…"

His words were cut off when he suddenly disappeared under the water. An ear piercing howl echoed through the room and I froze in terror. Ratchets.

A burst of water exploded from the liquid floor then four large ratchets landed in the prison room with a thud. They shook their heads as though ridding themselves of excess water before snarling and snapping at each of us. What happened to Abhainn?

Kain immediately thrust out his arm and focused on the ratchet closest to him. Hopefully he was using his water control to fight the creature. Brendan ran forward in just a few steps and launched himself on the back of the second ratchet. The sprite twisted and clamped his jaws together trying to get a bite of the selkie. Their moves seemed like a choreographed dance, until the ratchet pulled them both under the water. Since Brendan wasn't in his seal form, he wouldn't be able to breathe.

I lurched forward to reach for him, but something clamped onto my shoulder. I turned to see a ratchet staring up at me, ready to pounce again. He bit me and that was unacceptable. I prepared myself to attack him when a tendril of water leapt out of the floor and wrapped around the creature's neck. It screeched and fought, but in a matter of seconds, the ratchet was dead.

Graham made a horrible noise I could only describe as a moan. He'd used his water control to kill that ratchet and now it seemed as if he was paying the price. On his knees and hunched over, Graham coughed and sputtered, trying to catch his breath. I crouched down beside him and wrapped my arm across his back. He just saved me at the cost of his own health.

"Hold on, Graham. I'm going to get you out of here," I said and hoped it was true. A few more bodies slammed into the walls and a selkie was tossed through the door. I looked up to see Julian and Malcolm fighting hand to hand against my guards. Brendan pulled himself out of the water, gasping for air and bleeding from his arm.

"You have to find out what he wants," Graham muttered between breaths.

"What?" I asked not having a clue what he was talking about.

"Lucian…he's going to do something…you need to find out…to…stop." He continued to cough and I swear that I saw blood spray from his mouth. "He won't hurt you." I barely understood that last part.

"Graham!" I tried to get him to sit up, but he pushed me away.

"I'm okay, tart." He looked up at me with a smirk. Even though the situation was grim, his smile was addicting. "Nice to see that you care."

I rolled my eyes and stood to survey the battle in the room. Abhainn was back and had the last of the ratchets by the jaw, ripping it in two different directions. With a sickening crack, the sprite's head ripped in two. Abhainn tossed the body back into the water and wiped his hands. His attention was on the doorway where our three selkies were fighting with two more guards. In no time at all, Julian had them subdued and unconscious. I noticed how he didn't kill them.

"We 'ave to go," Abhainn said. "I'll leave this way, but the rest of ye will 'ave to head fer the beach. Isabel and I will meet ye there." He sunk beneath the surface before any of us had a chance to respond.

"We'll make sure it's clear," Julian said. He and Malcolm nodded toward Brendan then walked out the door.

Kain extended his hand. "Eviana, let's go."

Ignoring him, I finally looked directly at Brendan. "Please help him up." Without hesitation, Brendan came to my aide even though I saw the questions in his eyes. There were hundreds of inquiries to be had amongst us, but none were going to be addressed today.

Brendan wrapped his arm under Graham's shoulders and lifted him to his feet. "So, you're the selkie," Graham squeezed out between gritted teeth, obviously in pain from the movement.

Brendan glared at him but didn't respond. Instead he looked at me. "Please take him with you," I whispered, still speechless at the site of my ex-boyfriend here in front of me.

"Is this what you want?" Brendan asked. It seemed to have a double meaning.

"Yes. Make sure you get him back to the Council." Graham's head snapped up but I held my finger over his lips. "You need to tell them everything."

"Eviana…" It was one of the few times he'd used my real name.

"Adele will understand." I leaned forward and rested my hand on his cheek. He pushed his head into my touch and closed his eyes. Again, lacking any sort of impulse control, I bent in and gave him a quick kiss on the lips. "They will appreciate your honesty."

Graham smiled and I thought I saw something cross his face that resembled regret more than gratitude. But before I could place it, he and Brendan shuffled out the door and disappeared from my sight. I sucked in a big breath and sighed.

"Eviana?" Kain was still waiting patiently for me, but he knew something was going on.

I swallowed the fear in my throat and faced him. "I can't leave yet."

"What?"

"I need to know more. It's the only way to stop him." My shaking hands betrayed the false confidence I was trying to exude. Kain rushed to my side.

"No." He kept shaking his head. "No. I won't let you. You can't leave me again." Although his words sounded slightly controlling and possessive, they made my heart melt. Kain grabbed my face between his hands. "I can't lose you."

A single tear fell from my eye and I smiled. His touch sent electricity through my body like a lightning storm at sea. For years, I never allowed myself to let Kain in. Never gave him the chance. And now, in one night, it was abundantly clear how much we meant to each other. How much he meant to me.

"Kain, I have to. My family…it's connected to this group of leaders who want the war. Lucian was just beginning to tell me everything." I tried to put all of the words racing through my mind into some kind of cohesive thought. "He won't hurt me. Not anymore."

"Anymore?" Kain dropped his hands to his side and balled them into fists. "He kidnapped you. Stole you against your will. You can't stay here with him."

I reached for his hands and squeezed them tightly in mine. "Just a little longer. There is a Council meeting in two days. Meet me there and I will leave with you. That should be enough time..."

"Enough time for what?" he asked.

"For me to discover which leaders are on his side and figure out how we can defeat him. Some of the Council is with him, Kain. We can't prevent this war if we don't even know who we're fighting."

"What about your clan, Eviana? They need you." His forehead wrinkled in despair. He wasn't kidding when he said that he didn't want to let me go.

"This is what's best for them. It's the only way I can help. He won't hurt me." I realized then that I was going to have to tell him everything. My breath caught and it took several tries for me to speak again. "I'm his daughter."

Kain's mouth dropped open. He placed his hands on my shoulders so that he could get a good look at my face. "What?"

I swallowed hard. "It's true. My mother never told me. That's why he's been insisting that I join him. We share the same blood." I thought about how Graham and I had a bloodline that was instinctually attracted to each other. But then I looked at Kain. Instincts may win over some, but the feelings we had for each other took a lifetime to build and that made our connection all that much stronger. My stomach did a little flip flop at that realization.

"I...I don't know what to say," Kain stuttered. I pulled his arms around my waist so that we were as close as possible.

"You need to say that you will go tonight and take care of Graham. He is the only other one who knows. Use him to convince Adele and the others not to succumb to Lucian's commands. He's planning something...some kind of attack. I need more time to find out what it is."

"But what will he do to you when he sees that Graham escaped? You may be his daughter, but he's still a ruthless bastard."

I rose up on the tips of my toes and kissed him. "Thank you," I whispered.

"For what?"

"For trusting that I can handle this."

"I didn't say I was leaving," he replied with a little bit of an edge. "I want you to come with me." I kissed him again. "And your affections are not going to persuade me." His voice was light but he refused to break eye contact.

My emotions had negotiated the gauntlet of feelings this evening. I was ecstatic that my friends came to rescue me, elated that I had a chance to leave, concerned about my obligation to discover more about Lucian's plot, and euphoric with the realization of how much I loved Kain. And looking into his eyes, feeling his warm body pressed against mine, I knew that this was our beginning.

"No?" Another quick kiss on his soft, moist lips. "I think I can be pretty persuasive." I reached up to touch him again, but he pulled away and shook his head.

"Eviana, I can't do this. I can't leave you here. Not now." He turned away from me and walked into the shadows. "Do you have any idea what you're doing to me?"

I stepped next to him and grabbed his hand. He still kept his body facing the opposite direction. "Kain, just two more days. And then we can start our life together." What that meant exactly, I didn't know. But I felt those words come out of my mouth and I knew that I this is what I wanted; Kain and I to fight together, rule together, and be together. Just as it had always been planned.

He looked at me with such love, that it nearly broke my concentration. In one swift motion, he grabbed me by the waist and lifted me up against him. His mouth covered mine and I didn't hold back. I wrapped my legs around his sides and enjoyed the feel of every part of his body. I'd heard that stressful situations could lead to extreme behavior, but what surged through my body was so much more than adrenaline. It was passion, desire, completeness. Everything I thought I'd lost when Brendan walked out of my life. If we weren't in such a dire circumstance right now, I think we could have behaved this way all night long.

At some point we stopped making out like our life depended on it and hugged each other tight. I shed silent tears, hoping that I was once again making the right decision. In my gut, I knew that I was. But in my heart, I never wanted to let go of Kain.

I slid back down to the floor and pushed him toward the door. "Go."

Although Kain was naked and very exposed, he stood there in total confidence. This is what a true leader was. He had an aura about him that I could only hope to emulate. "I hate doing this."

"I know," I said. "But it's only for two more days."

He ran his hands through his shaggy blond hair. "I wish I knew why you had so much power over me." At first I thought he was upset, but when I saw his brilliant smile and sparkling eyes, I knew the question had been rhetorical.

"Go," I whispered.

Without saying another word, he ran through the door and down the path to the beach. I watched him go with a heavy heart. I hoped they would be okay. I hoped that they would all survive.

When Kain reached the edge of my sight line, he turned and looked at me. I lifted a hand in acknowledgment, aware of how much it trembled. I didn't want him to leave. He waved and then ran around the bend, disappearing into the darkness.

I remembered the night before our wedding when I said goodbye to him for what I thought was going to be the last time. Tonight, I wished he could stay next to me forever. I had to believe this wouldn't be the last time we saw each other.

With many of the selkies still asleep or knocked out cold, I didn't think it would take long for Lucian to discover what had happened. Resolving myself to face what was coming, I left the prison door opened and waited inside on the floor as my heart continued to pound and my stomach fluttered like a trapped bird.

I really hoped that Lucian wouldn't harm me.

Thirteen

Kain

Leaving her hurt worse than being skewered by Lucian's sword. I wasn't even sure how I walked away from her at all. There must have been a part of me that knew this was what needed to be done, otherwise I surprised myself with my actions.

And what about the way she responded to me? I still couldn't believe what had happened. My heart swelled with love just thinking about her lips. For so long, I wanted this for us. And for so long I feared that it was a lost cause. But now it was really happening. We had a chance to make our lives fit together in every sense of the word and I could barely hold back the grin on my face.

Then it hit me. How could I leave her when I felt so strongly? When *she* felt so strongly? I had to go back.

I turned away from the surf and made it a few steps before stopping. No. I needed to trust that she knew what had to be done.

She wasn't injured and she swore he wouldn't do anything to harm her. She was his daughter after all.

His daughter. That still didn't sit right with me, and I hoped that I could find out more from Graham. Lucian Sutherland had to be the most obnoxious, repulsive merman of us all and Eviana was part of his own flesh and blood. It was frightening to think about. But I also knew Eviana as a person, as a leader, and a friend. They may share the same blood, but she most certainly was not her father's daughter.

Just before reaching the water, I saw several heads beyond the breaking waves. Troy beckoned me to hurry up, but one of the seals swam closer to the shore. I watched him look up and down the beach and then glare at me. Before he slid out of his fur, I knew that Brendan wasn't happy.

"Where is she?" he demanded. "Where. Is. She?" This time, it was accompanied by a not so subtle push against my shoulders. I stumbled back and tried to catch myself, causing me to realize that most of the pain from my injury was finally gone. "If you left her there, I swear I will kill you!"

"She has a plan," I said, holding my hand up to warn him away. "We have to trust her."

"How can you say that?" Brendan ran toward me, his green eyes glimmering with rage. "I have to get her!"

"No, you don't. She won't go with you." I watched his face curl in disgust.

"Just like she wouldn't go with you?"

"She doesn't want to see you and I know what I'm doing." It took every ounce of respect I had for Eviana not to get in his face. He had no right dictating Eviana's life.

"You don't know shit," he spat. Moving so that we were inches apart, he pushed his finger into my chest. "Just because she was happy to see you tonight does not mean she will want anything to do with you later."

"Get your hand off me," I snarled, surprised at the intensity in my voice. The adrenaline was rapidly taking over.

"You can't order me around." He stepped past me toward the boat house. "Just like you can't stop me from rescuing Eviana."

I didn't think, just reacted. The moment he took one step in that direction, I pounced. Pushing him to the ground, I used my body weight to hold Brendan's face against the sand. He struggled, but I held tight. "You have to let her do this. For once, stay out of her life."

Brendan suddenly pushed upward and tossed me off to the side. I found myself on my back with his arm pressed tightly across my throat. I managed to get my hands underneath his forearm, but he was strong. We were pretty equally matched.

"I'm not going to sit back and watch you take her from me, fish. I may not be able to have a life with her anymore, but neither will you." The heat from his breath only infuriated me more.

We rolled in the sand two more times before I was able to break free. Jumping to my feet, I prepared to fight him head on. "So what? You're going to kill me, dog?" *Just try it*, I thought to myself.

Brendan came after me again with a fist that I dodged and countered. My hand landed against the side of his ribs and he yelled in pain before I felt my legs fall out from underneath me. On my back again, Brendan wrapped his hands around my throat. I punched at the side of his head, but he wouldn't let go. His eyes glowered with craziness.

Suddenly, his body flew away from me and I sucked in a deep, cleansing breath. "Get up!" Julian commanded at me. "You two have attracted too much attention."

He stepped over me and walked to Brendan who was now sitting on his knees waiting for his punishment. It was such a strange submissive behavior. I really needed to find out who Julian really was and why he wielded so much power over the selkies.

"Kain?" Troy called to me from the surf. "Is everything okay?"

I lifted my hand in acknowledgement. "Yes, I'm coming."

Brendan and Julian slipped back into their skins and swam to the boat away from the rest of us. I joined Troy who told me Palmer and Graham had already started the trip. We passed Isabel and Abhainn under the water along with a dozen new ratchets who appeared to be in Isabel's favor. As we moved out of sight, I heard the clashing of teeth and bodies as the ratchets continued protecting us from the selkie guards and others of their kind.

I was grateful for the physical relief from fighting, but my mind was still seething with anger. So much of me wanted to get rid of Brendan once and for all, yet the adult in me knew it was a hasty reaction. I didn't have the luxury of acting on impulses. If I did, things would be much easier in my life. Especially the decision to leave Eviana behind.

We reached the boat without encountering any more attacks. Surprising, considering this was Lucian we were dealing with. Palmer and Graham had already shifted back to full human form and were waiting on the boat. I watched the three selkies launch themselves from the water, each landing hard on the bow but successful in their attempt. They quickly pulled out of their skins and slid on pieces of their clothing.

Troy and I kicked our way into the boat, my legs transitioning before I even finished the move. It appeared that my clan leader perks were back in full swing. Abhainn surfaced without Isabel and I checked his face to see if something was wrong.

He smiled. "Thank ye fer yer concern, lad. But she is going to stay with her kind fer a while. They 'ave some catching up to do." Abhainn floated up out of the water and hovered over the boat for a moment before gently lowering into the driver's seat. "Where is Eviana?" he asked, looking all around.

"He left her," Brendan growled.

"What?" Graham and Palmer asked at the same time.

"I will see her again in a few days. She has her reasons and we all need to trust that she knows what she's doing." I directed my comment to Brendan, but it was Abhainn who spoke next.

"Interesting."

"What's interesting?" I asked.

He waved his hand and started the boat engine. "Nothing to be concerned with, lad."

We jerked forward and I nearly fell off the side as Abhainn turned us around. Someone pulled on my shoulder.

"Why did she stay?" Graham yelled into my ear over the noise of the engine.

"She said that she needed to find out more from Lucian." I looked at him square in the face. "And I'd also like to talk to you about that as well."

Graham smirked and then glanced off into the distance. Something about his reaction bothered me, even though I couldn't place exactly what it was. I think it was almost as if he expected it.

I noticed Palmer sitting with a blanket wrapped around his shoulders and a paleness to his skin that I hadn't seen before. "Are you okay?" I asked.

He tried to smile. "Are you sure this is the right thing to do?"

I knew he was worried, and rightly so. He was his cousin's primary protector. "Yes. And when we get on the plane, I will explain everything to you." I patted his shoulder and he nodded. Palmer was a loyal friend.

The surprisingly calm water cooperated with our escape for most of the ride. But as we got about halfway back to the mainland, the swells increased and we were forced to slow to idle speed.

"What's going on?" I asked Abhainn, who was concentrating on his driving. He shook his head. "Do you think we should just swim?"

"Aye, perhaps that would be better." He motioned for us to jump overboard. Swimming under that water was much easier in a storm than swimming on the surface.

I looked up into the sky and wondered if there was something else going on. Not one single cloud hid the millions of stars and there was very little breeze. Why did the ocean turn so rough?

As if answering my question, Graham suddenly stood and thrust his arms out to the side. Almost immediately, the water split around the boat and curved up to join in the center above our heads. We were surrounded.

"Good idea, Master Forrester," Palmer said with a smile. It appeared Graham had subdued the waves.

But then I saw the expression on Graham's face. Something was off and it sent a shiver down my spine. He threw his arm up into the air and I watched in horror as a giant wave slammed into the front of the boat, knocking every selkie overboard. In another quick move, Graham managed to wrap Abhainn in a water tunnel, effectively freezing him in place. Abhainn's face mirrored the horror of my own when we both realized that we had been duped.

Palmer attempted to attack Graham, but just as he was about to touch him, he screamed out in pain and grasped his head. Falling to his knees, Palmer was helpless as he rocked back and forth in the boat.

Graham looked at me. "Why are you doing this?" I asked. "She trusted you!" I attempted to fight against his water control by throwing a wave or two at him myself. It knocked him around, but he still maintained his grip on Abhainn and Palmer. Two tendrils of water shot out from the top of our aqueous tunnel and grabbed Troy's legs. They lifted him up and pulled his body in opposite directions until his screams pierced through every one of us.

"Stop this!" I yelled, pushing my own water control onto Graham. It was enough for him to drop his hold on Troy, but the merman fell back into the boat and I thought I heard something crack in his neck. He landed hard and he didn't move.

"I am going to leave here and you are not going to follow me." I thought Graham was talking to me, but then noticed that he was looking at the three selkies who were trying to climb back on board. "If these guys make any attempt to come after me, you will kill them. Do you understand?"

A chorus of affirmatives filled the night. Graham had control of everyone on this boat in one way or another. He was as powerful as Lucian if not more. Why did Eviana want to help him?

"What about her?"

"Who?" Graham asked nonchalantly as he squeezed Abhainn a little tighter. This was every sprite's worst fear; being trapped in the water by a merman.

"Eviana! She wanted you to help us." I tried to move closer to Graham, but stopped when he looked at me.

"Uh, uh. Not one more step or I will have these selkies tear into each and every one of you. However, not before I squeeze the life out of this one," he said nodding at Abhainn, "and make his head explode," he finished with a look at Palmer.

"We will come after you," I snarled.

"I have no doubt," Graham said with an arrogance unmatched by anyone other than Lucian. "Tell Eviana I will be expecting her."

With that, Graham dropped the tunnel and flooded the entire boat with a thousand pounds of water. It landed hard on top of us and

I tried to cover Palmer with my body the best I could. Abhainn yelled and dove on top of Troy who was still completely unconscious. By the time the wash of water subsided, only the seven of us remained. Graham was long gone.

"Dammit," Julian cursed and let out a frustrated sigh. It had to be hard for them to be so susceptible to merfolk compulsion.

"What was that all about?" Brendan asked, coughing and spitting excess water from his lungs.

"It appears Master Forrester was a part of this all along," Abhainn snarled.

"Do you think he's going back to her?" I asked.

"No. This was part of a plan. He will not return to the island." Abhainn sounded so sure of himself. He stood in the center of the boat and helped Troy to his knees. Thankfully he wasn't hurt too bad. "We have to abandoned ship."

"Huh?" Palmer asked, rubbing the sides of his head. I still didn't know what Graham had done to him. It wasn't possible for merfolk to control each other. Or was it?

Abhainn gestured to the front of the boat which was quickly taking on water due to the excess weight from Graham's wave. Gathering what bags were still within reach, we jumped into the water and continued to the mainland.

I thought about what just happened. Lucian didn't appear to be the only powerful one, and when Eviana mentioned that Council members were involved, I wondered if she realized just how right she had been.

I wouldn't let her go to that Council meeting alone. I was going to be there and I would make sure that she came home with me this time.

Fourteen

Eviana

Hours passed. Or maybe time slowed while I waited for someone to realize what had happened. I could hear the selkies stirring, at least those that were still lying in the boat house with me. No more ratchets appeared to intimidate me, which made me think they were pursuing my rescue team.

A huge wave of relief swept through my bones. They'd found me. Despite what Lucian said, I still had friends and family who cared enough to get me away from him. I didn't need the Council. I had Kain and Abhainn. And Brendan.

The sudden stab of guilt hit me with an unexpected punch. What did I have to feel guilty about? He's the one who left me. I was allowed to move on. But then he also came back and risked his life for me. I wanted to be mad at Brendan for all of the pain and torment he put me through. Doubting myself and wondering why I wasn't enough had wrecked havoc on my mind and soul. To be discarded so easily…that was a tough notion to get over. Brendan didn't think I was sufficient for him but Kain never stopped loving me.

Kain. Excitement swirled in my stomach at the thought of what we just shared. He'd always accepted me and even though I wasn't perfect, his belief in me never wavered. I still didn't know why it had taken me so long to understand all of this. Kain and I should be together. It's what our families always wanted. It's what was best for our clans. It's what was *right*.

I couldn't help but cry when I thought about what my mother would be thinking right now. "Finally," she'd probably say. Then my dad would give me a hug that made me feel safe and loved. He always was the more nurturing one of the two. Perhaps that's because of my mother's family. Now that I knew a bit about her history, I suddenly felt sad for her being forced into a life that she didn't want. Although she did choose my father, much to the dismay of her own.

We were much more alike than I'd ever realized.

Exhausted from crying and fighting, I wished that someone would hurry up and find me. Going back to the house didn't seem like the right option. I needed Lucian to know that I chose to stay behind. It might help my chances of survival.

A muffled voice snapped me out of my thoughts. "Get up!" it commanded. Almost at once, the selkies on the floor began to move. The smallest one rubbed his head in confusion before focusing on me. His green eyes filled with anger while he curled his lip up into a snarl. I unconsciously slid away from him, not even thinking to reach for my powers.

Pulling himself up to his hands and knees, he crawled toward me like a hunting cat. I looked toward the other two selkies for help, but they were still trying to orient themselves.

"Back up," I said a little too weakly, so I threw up my hands in front of me to ward him off. Clearing my throat, I tried again. "Stay away from me!" The selkie growled, an odd sound coming from a human.

"Enough!" Lucian demanded the second he stepped through the boat house door. "Leave us and gather the rest."

It was as though the selkie flipped a switch in his brain. One second he was a snarling, fighting animal ready to kill me, and the next he was a docile servant. The selkie nodded to Lucian and helped lift his buddies off the floor. I stayed crouched in the corner, trapped between the watery cage and my evil father hovering in the doorway.

Focusing on the retreating selkies, I tried not to look at Lucian. My heart thudded in my chest, anticipating the worst response. So when he smiled at me, I should have felt relieved. But the thin line of his lips and the hollow look in his eyes frightened me to no end.

"You're here," he said coolly. I could only nod my head. The lump I was trying to swallow held on for dear life. "I am surprised."

"I decided to stay," I managed to whisper.

"I see that." He walked a few steps closer and put his hands on his hips as he looked around the room. "And Master Forrester?"

I forced myself to stand, angry with my legs for being so shaky. "He's gone."

"Gone?" he asked in amusement.

"Yes, he's going back to the Council to tell them everything."

Lucian laughed. It was dark and evil and it made my skin crawl. "Oh, I am sure that he will." He reached for me. "This pleases me very much."

I had just taken a step closer to Lucian when I froze. "What are you talking about? Did you even hear what I said? He's going to tell them everything. You're finished with this stupid war."

Again, he cackled like a witch stirring her magic cauldron. "Far from it, daughter. Come now. We have many preparations to make before the meeting."

"I'm not going anywhere until you tell me what's going on." And like a stubborn two year old, I slammed my foot on the ground and crossed my arms.

Lucian sighed. "You really need to represent yourself better." He moved to the door. "I will explain inside. I'm starving and I want to eat."

He left the room without looking back, assuming I would follow. I guess I didn't really have much of a choice. He didn't seem to be angry with me, in fact his reaction was rather docile. Maybe I would survive until the Council meeting after all.

Lucian sauntered along the sandy path with a trail of selkies following behind. Many of them were limping or holding a part of their body that had been injured. Selkies had always been dear to me, however, these ones picked the wrong side. Granted, many of them were consistently under Lucian's control, but he didn't force them here in the first place. They'd sided with a monster.

The sinister ocean slammed against the shoreline, creating rough surf and enough noise to almost drown out my thoughts.

Although when I realized this, I also noticed the sudden lack of heads patrolling the liquid perimeter. The ratchets were missing. I personally saw two of them die and I imagined Abhainn did his fair share in hurting the rest. The evil twin in me smiled.

Upon reaching the house, Lucian dismissed the selkies, telling them to fix their wounds and rest up. He and I passed through the joined living and dining area out to the back patio. It was dark and late, but my adrenaline spiked as I waited for our conversation to begin.

Pulling two wicker lounge chairs together, Lucian gestured for me to sit. "Snacks will arrive soon. Can I get you something to drink?"

I hesitated. Why was he being so nice to me after what just happened? "Water, please."

He smiled and jerked his chin. The little selkie women stuck her head out of the sliding glass door and focused on Lucian while he gave her our orders. I wonder how she felt about only using her selkie abilities for maid duties. It must be frustrating.

"So, you decided to stay? How intriguing." He paused for a moment and stared out at the sea. Even though there wasn't a moon, his blond hair glowed. As much as I hated to admit it, there was something mesmerizing about him. That sentiment creeped me out immediately.

"I wanted to hear more about your plan," I said.

"My *plan*? My plan for what?"

"World domination," I replied and he laughed.

"Well, this little escapade tonight was a part of it. Step two of my evil agenda begins at the Council meeting." I couldn't tell if he was being sarcastic or not.

"You do realize Graham escaped and my friends tried to rescue me, right?" I asked, not liking the nonchalant way he was handling this conversation.

"*Tried* being the opportune word here. Yes, I know this. Graham was supposed to escape, although I am disappointed with the mass exodus of the sprites. I wasn't anticipating that."

Ignoring the ratchet comment for a moment, I focused on the important part of his words. "Graham was *supposed* to escape? What are you talking about, Lucian?"

He looked over at me then. At first his expression was one of annoyance but it quickly shifted into surprise. I watched his eyes twinkle and his jaw drop. "Are you really that naive?"

"Lucian…" I pleaded with him to get on with it.

"My, it seems as if I need to give Master Forrester credit where credit is due. He had you completely fooled."

A sickening pit opened in the bottom of my stomach. Replaying every beating, conversation, and meeting amongst the two or three of us, I couldn't help but shake my head. "He was a prisoner too. You beat him!"

"First of all, you are not a prisoner…" He held up his hand when I tried to protest. "And second, Graham agreed to the beatings."

"What?"

"He said that it needed to look authentic or you would never buy it. I must admire how well he knows your psyche. You really are a good match for each other."

The selkie returned at that moment to deliver chips and guacamole. My appetite was long gone and the second she went back inside, I started grilling him.

"I don't believe you. You will say anything to have the upper hand. You're just mad that we figured out how to get away from you." I ground my teeth together to hold back some of the anger. And the growing deception I felt toward Graham.

"You didn't all get away," he said and raised his eyebrows. "And this was my plan from the beginning."

"Graham wouldn't do that to me," I whispered, suddenly aware of how small I felt.

"No?" Lucian asked.

"No."

"It always amazes me how much physical attraction can blind natural instincts. Your mother and I were like that. When the bloodline desires a mate, it is hard to see their flaws."

"He's been tainted by your schemes," I said surprised I was defending Graham when he'd done nothing but hurt me.

Lucian laughed again. Biting into a chip, I watched a piece of guacamole fall from his mouth. It reminded me of all of those he hurt; one wrong move and you'll be consumed. Forever trapped in his world or digested and expelled like the waste. This man could not rule our kind. I needed to figure out how to stop him.

"Why did you say that the drugs were setting me free?" The sudden change in topic seemed to catch him off guard if the stunned look on his face was any indication. Lucian rarely broke his composure.

"Because they are. Your mother's refusal to teach you anything has left me with little choice. I am running out of time and this is the only way to make up for eighteen years of neglect." He sipped what I assumed was a margarita with its lime shade and salted rim. Smacking his lips together, he continued. "Can you feel it taking effect yet?"

"No! I told you that it makes me feel weak."

He looked at me for a long moment. Stared into my soul. "You're almost there. Just a few more days."

Days? In a few days I hoped to be back home in California with my family and Kain. Another round of butterflies danced in my stomach and warmed my body with love. I was so ready to get home and start this new life together with him. We already ruled as one, now we could *be* one.

"Eviana?" Lucian interrupted my daydream.

"Huh?"

"Did you hear what I said?"

"No." Not that I really cared.

"I told you that you will need to get past your aversion for what Graham has done. I think he really, genuinely cares for you." Lucian's tone seemed sincere.

"I don't care. I want to know what you're doing to me. Why do you have to 'set me free'?" I used air quotes to enhance my sarcasm.

He remained silent for a long time and I thought that maybe I blew it. I'd stayed behind so that I could learn more about his plans and personality so that the rest of my kind could defeat him. And now, I may have messed it up.

"Do you recall what I said yesterday? About there being others more powerful than me?" I was surprised that this is the direction he went. "You have that potential, Eviana. As a product of your mother's and my love, you inherited a tremendous amount of power. There aren't very many like you out there."

I chose to ignore the love part. "But I'm not anywhere near where you and Graham are when it comes to water control or compulsion."

"You will be. Soon."

"Why?" Not that the idea wasn't intriguing, but I needed to know why it mattered.

Lucian didn't answer at first. "It was always your birthright. Not to be just a clan leader, but to be a leader of all kinds. Merfolk, selkies, sprites, humans…there are only a few who can do it."

I didn't know what to say. I certainly didn't want to rule over every living creature in this world. Is this what Lucian had planned all along?

As if answering my question he added, "I can't do it alone."

"I won't follow The Legacy."

"You will do more than that, Eviana. You will make everyone believe in its effectiveness and necessity. And you will do this very soon."

"Stop trying to tell me what I will and won't do. I am not one of your selkies." I was so irritated with his arrogance and sureness of his master schemes.

"You are much more than a selkie to me. You will understand that shortly." He stretched back in his chair and yawned. "Well, it's been an eventful evening and now I shall retire to my room."

"I'm not finished with this conversation," I said and stood.

"I am. Goodnight, daughter." He quickly reached forward and kissed the top of my head before I could pull away.

His ridiculous silk shirt billowed out behind him as he made his way inside. I was left alone to wallow in my thoughts. Lucian's mind worked within a system that I couldn't interpret, and that worried me to no end. What was he planning? Why was I the key to his success?

In two days, we would meet with the Council. I'd finally discover what he was up to and then I would leave with Kain. Until then, I needed to play along and learn what I could. I needed to survive.

Fifteen

Eviana

Unfortunately, I couldn't discover anything about Lucian when he disappeared. As soon as I awoke each day, I looked all over for my estranged father. Much to my disappointment, I was told that he was out, but I knew that he was hiding. He didn't want to speak to me before the Council meeting. I don't know why exactly, but I just knew that was true.

We arrived at the Dallas/Fort Worth airport shortly before sunset. I'd never been to Texas before, and although Dallas seemed like a sprawling city, I wasn't a fan of the dry heat we encountered on our way to the meeting. Instead of a hotel, we were driving to a country club. Where better to ensure exclusivity and privacy for a secret merfolk meeting? Apparently one of the clan's had a long history with the club and when requested, they got anything they needed.

Lucian forced me to dress in a ridiculous gown. It wasn't that the design was horrible, quite the opposite actually. The long, form fitting indigo dress complimented my hair, and the slit up the side of my right leg was sure to draw attention. It was strapless and surprisingly quite comfortable. I had to wear long gloves that reached the top of my elbows, and despite my best protests, Lucian demanded that I wrap my hair up off my neck and into a bun. His obsession with the way I looked made the whole ordeal quite ludicrous to me. That, and I knew I would look like a trophy on his arm.

Sparkling lights and fiery torches lit the path up to the main entrance of the club. The ancient oaks hovered over the road like an embrace. Branches reached and crawled toward each other effectively creating a tunnel of foliage. We sat on opposite sides in the back of a black limousine, since Lucian insisted on making a dramatic appearance. His dark blue suit complimented my dress and he even pulled his long blond hair back into a ponytail. We looked like a couple of movies stars begging for attention. Exactly what I didn't want.

"You will behave tonight," Lucian suddenly said.

"I'm not three," I snapped.

"No, but sometimes you act like it." It was such an insulting, fatherly thing to say. He had no right. But before I could protest, he continued. "You will only speak when asked a direct question. Do you understand?"

I didn't say anything. He didn't deserve an answer.

"If you do not obey, I promise you there will be consequences," he said.

"What, like you'll beat up Graham some more? No one is left for you to use against me."

At least I hoped that there wasn't. All I needed to do was get inside and find Kain. I wanted to find out more about Lucian's plans, but I hoped that we would get enough information from the meeting tonight. I assumed that he was going to place some kind of demand on the table. Would it involve me? I didn't doubt that it would. The Council hadn't been real anxious to help save me. Perhaps that would be his angle. They back off completely and he stops the senseless killings.

As much as that would be the ideal situation, I sincerely doubted it would ever happen. Lucian wouldn't honor a truce, but he still might convince them otherwise. These were leaders of the American and international Councils. If they had an opportunity to make a deal in the name of peace, I bet they would take it. Regardless of my situation.

Then suddenly, I had a panicked thought. Not about the Council all but signing me over to Lucian, but about Kain and his role tonight. This would for sure be a closed meeting, privy to only those deemed fit. Would Kain be one of them? He and Adele had worked closely together over the past several months, but Kain wasn't a Council member. My breath caught in my throat in the complete terror that I wouldn't be able to leave with him tonight.

Then I remembered who I was thinking about. Kain wouldn't leave me this time. He would find a way to free me from my father's grasp no matter what it entailed. Kain was reliable.

"Eviana?" Lucian asked and his tone implied it wasn't the first time he spoke. His hand extended into the limo, waiting for me to join him outside. "It's time."

I placed my gloved hand in his and let him help me out of the car. *Must play along*, I reminded myself. The hot night air seemed stuffy and suffocating. Or maybe that was just my life.

I took a few steps forward, thankful for that slit in the dress. Three club employees greeted us, followed by four protectors. They belonged to the Council, and I watched closely as they eyed up Lucian and me.

"Sir," the apparent leader of the security team said. "They may wait outside." He was referring to the two selkies Lucian brought with us. There were more here, just staying out of sight.

Lucian pushed past the protector as though he were an annoying insect. "They come with me."

"But sir…" the man said. Lucian stopped so suddenly, he nearly yanked my arm off. He stared at the merman and narrowed his eyes. My head began to hurt.

"You will not speak to me again, nor will you prevent any of my security team from entering this building. Nod if you understand." He bobbed his head up down like a marionette. "Excellent," Lucian finished. He turned and pulled me through the doors, the selkies following closely behind.

Lucian was an incredible threat. He just controlled one of his own without breaking a sweat. We weren't supposed to be able to do that. Although both he and Graham tried it on me, I thought maybe it wasn't possible since they hadn't succeeded. Now I realized how badly

I'd misjudged his abilities. Another round of nerves prickled over my skin. I really needed to get away from him.

It appeared the most of the club was closed to the regular members as only merfolk filled the meeting area. A few were dressed in long gold, dark green, or black robes symbolizing their presence on an international Council. These ruling organizations were littered all over the world, with several on each continent. Well, except for Australia who only had one Council, and Antarctica where no merfolk resided at all. I didn't see any of the maroon cloaked members representing the North American Council.

But I did see someone else.

"I'm going to the ladies room," I said polite and sweet to Lucian, and loud enough for others to here. Certainly he couldn't deny me that request. He smiled and dropped his arm, allowing me to move by myself. Freedom. For at least a few moments.

"Don't be too long. We are about to make our announcement," he added. What announcement? The sheer look of malice in his eyes made my legs shake in fear. So much was riding on tonight going smoothly, and yet Lucian wouldn't think twice about disrupting everyone's plan.

We were here for him. He'd convinced the Council to bring those that best represented each clan so that he could discuss the next steps with them. It was reasonable, and he pretended to go along with the charade. But in reality, they would be fools to think he didn't have an ulterior motive.

As did I. Making my way around the corner and out of his sight, I noticed a door slowly closing. Running as discretely as I could,

I reached the men's bathroom a few seconds later. Nice. I looked up and down the hallway and quickly pressed my back against the door to slip inside. Hopefully no one else would follow me in.

There was a second entrance, and as soon as I pushed through, my heart rate increased and my mouth turned up in a smile too big for me to control. Kain waited there with arms outstretched, a smile as big as my own reflecting back at me.

"You're here," I said and jumped into his embrace. I felt him laugh and squeeze me tighter.

"There was no way Adele could stop me," he said. "Plus she owed me after what I told her about Graham."

My muscles stiffened at the mention of his name. "I'm so sorry Kain. I didn't know."

He kissed my forehead with the lightest of touch. "I know. We didn't get very far before he revealed himself."

"Was anyone hurt?" I asked, suddenly remembering what Graham could do. I was fairly certain that he faked the loss of his powers among the many other things he'd lied about.

"Troy got it the worst, and he took control of the selkies. But Abhainn was the one who is the most upset." He looked down into my eyes and moved his hands to the side of my face. "It doesn't matter though. You're here and you're coming home with me."

Those words had so many different meanings, that if I hadn't noticed the desire in his eyes, I could have misinterpreted it. He wanted me to come home with him, but not in a protective kind of way. No, it was much more intimate than that.

I closed my eyes when I felt his lips press against mine. Once again, every errant thought disappeared and it was all I could do not to lose control. Reaching up, I grabbed his head in my hands and lost myself in the feel of his sun bleached hair. It was still longer than normal and I decided right then that I liked it that way.

My fingers caressed the strands while his hands travelled lower on my body. Much lower. I felt his timid brush against the slit in my dress that almost reached the top of my thigh. Goosebumps erupted all over my body and I shivered in anticipation. We had never been this close before.

And although we should have stopped, it was quite obvious that neither of us wanted to. When he pulled his lips away from mine, I almost screamed until I felt them again, moving down my neck. The strapless dress left plenty of kissable skin, and Kain hit every spot. Twice.

If I could have had a conscious thought, I would have wondered why I couldn't seem to get enough of him. It had only been a little more than a week since Brendan broke my heart, but those few days felt like a lifetime. So much had happened since then. So many lives had been lost or almost stolen from me. It took those experiences for me to realize what I truly wanted out of life and who I wanted in it. My heart swelled with so much love for Kain, I swear it was going to explode.

"Ah, if ye keep this up, we are going to 'ave to find ye a private room. And fast." Abhainn's voice scared me so much I bit Kain's lip.

"Oh no! I'm so sorry," I said, trying to reach for his face.

He wiped his mouth and chuckled when his hand came away with blood on it. "It's okay. Barely scratched the surface. Besides, you can do that any time you want."

I knew my face blushed, especially if Abhainn's snort was any indication. His foot high frame floated above the gold sink, where I presumed he had entered the facility. "I'm glad that yer 'aving a happy reunion, but we must be leaving soon. The place is crawling with security."

"We're leaving now?" I asked Kain, still standing a few feet away out of sheer embarrassment.

"It would be best. Adele told me that we should sneak you out during the hoopla that's sure to go on once the meeting starts."

I nodded my head, knowing that I should trust in them. "Okay then. Let's go." I was grateful for the Council leader's concern. Especially after they decided to leave me trapped at Lucian's.

"I'm afraid that won't be possible, daughter." Lucian stood in the doorway with a sinister look on his face and his left hand outstretched toward the sink. Abhainn made several choking sounds before falling silent. The sprite had his own hands around his throat and he appeared to be fighting with himself. He was suffocating.

"What are you doing to him?" I yelled.

"I'm controlling the water. Every molecule that makes up these creatures can be manipulated to do as I command. I find it amusing that the sprite is choking himself, don't you?" Abhainn's wide eyes appeared to double in size, and I feared they may pop out of his head.

"Kain, do something," I begged. His water control skills far surpassed mine. But the moment he acknowledged what I said, Lucian was on him. His fingers wrapped around Kain's throat and although the two men were equal in size, Lucian lifted him off the ground like he weighed nothing.

"It's a shame your parents held you back, too." Lucian looked up into Kain's eyes and cocked his head like a hawk eyeing up prey. "I can see the power in you. *Feel* it. Too bad you two won't have the chance to be together. What a commanding couple you'd be. Maybe even more so than my arrangement." Kain struggled against his hold and just as he was about to tear Lucian's hands away, the merman spoke. "Sleep."

Kain's body relaxed and Lucian dropped him to the floor with little regard. Abhainn gasped for air while fighting against his own hands.

"Please stop this!" I screamed. And then I got mad. Lucian was facing Kain so I leapt forward and jumped onto his back. It was difficult in the dress and I think I heard the slit tear higher up my leg.

Lucian spun around and slammed my back against the wall. The bone crushing blow forced all of the air out of my lungs, yet I still held on. He took a few steps forward and then ran back into the wall again. My head crashed along the marble tiles as he continued to beat my body. Within a few seconds, I couldn't hold on anymore. My grasp loosened and I fell to the floor.

"Finally," Lucian said, shrugging his shoulders and pulling his jacket back into place. "I've had quite enough of this." He flicked his hand at Abhainn and the sprite shattered into a thousand different pieces. The droplets plummeted into the sink and onto the counter. Unlike all of the other times I'd watch them move back together to form his body again, the water stayed still. In the next second, Lucian pulled Kain up by his throat and slapped him hard across the face with his free hand. I screamed again then covered my mouth when I saw Lucian's glare.

"Shut up!" He looked back to Kain who seemed to be waking up. "And be quiet or I end this now. I want both of you to listen carefully." Squeezing his throat, Lucian didn't give Kain an option. Kain's eyes found mine while Lucian simply glared at me. "If you don't stand with me before the Council tonight, I will kill him in the most horrible way you can imagine." To emphasize the threat he twisted his wrist and Kain's face turned red.

"Stop!" He'd already killed Abhainn, I believed Kain would be next. "Why are you doing this? What is wrong with you?"

He tossed Kain into the wall and marched over to me. Grabbing my upper arm, he yanked me to my feet. "I told you that you would convince the Council to follow The Legacy, and now I'm gathering my insurance." His mouth was so close to my face that I could feel his hot, angry breath. For the first time since all of this began, I was really, truly afraid of this man.

"How...how am I supposed to do that?" I could barely speak.

He started to push me toward the door. "You will tell them that you discovered the error in your ways, and now you see the need for us to take control."

I looked up at him with uncertainty. "But I don't feel that way. How am I supposed to convince them otherwise?"

Before I knew what happened, I felt my cheek burn and tasted blood in my mouth. Lucian had slapped me so hard, it took seconds before the pain settled in.

"You will obey me," he snarled. "You don't...he dies." Kain was trying to push himself up off the ground, so Lucian bounded over and kick him hard in the stomach. Tears began to flow down my face.

"Please, don't hurt him."

"Then do as I say, and don't even think about trying to leave here tonight." I nodded. Lucian would kill Kain. I didn't doubt it for one second. All of our plans to escape tonight and gather up those against Lucian and his ideals shattered like the sprite that had been my friend.

Someone slammed the outside bathroom door shut and we all froze. In the second I went to yell for help, my emotions evolved from hopeful to devastated to furious. Graham's perfectly healed face and designer suit made me want to scream.

"You!" I growled. "You have some nerve coming back here..."

"I missed you too, tart," he interrupted. "I'm so glad we can have this reunion. My life has been dreadful since I left your side in the arms of your selkie." His flippant attitude infuriated every cell in my body.

"You bastard!" It literally it felt like my blood was boiling inside my skin. If Lucian still hadn't had a tight hold on my arm, I would have attacked the traitor. Then I remembered what Kain said. "Oh. Have they seen you yet?" Graham lifted his eyebrows in question. "The Council's going to love to hear from you, especially since they know everything." My focus briefly turned to Kain struggling on the ground and Graham laughed.

"Are you referring to Adele? Yes, well, I'm afraid Mistress Lyonetta won't be spilling any secrets tonight."

My stomach plummeted and all of that blood seething at the surface, drained to my toes. What had they done to her?

"Enough of this. It is time," Lucian said. He yanked me forward and turned me so that I was facing Kain. Lucian's fingers dug into my shoulders, forcing me to look. "Remember, you will convince the Council to celebrate in our success or your precious boyfriend will die."

In that moment, Kain and I shared a look that spoke a thousand words. Love, devotion, fear, and obstinacy. Kain smiled at me and I knew that we weren't giving up just yet.

Graham walked over to Kain and picked him off the ground. Using his forearm, he pushed Kain against the wall. He looked back and forth between the two of us. "Ah come on, let me tell the bloke. Please?"

Lucian didn't respond. Instead, he made me step closer. I saw his head lean out past my right shoulder and then suddenly felt his left hand caressing my face. He spoke to Kain. "Say one word, alert one protector and I will take her away from you permanently."

Kain's eyes widened as he pushed against Graham. "You wouldn't hurt her," he said.

"No?" Both of Lucian's hands wrapped tightly around my head. I could feel him pushing into my mind, but instead of telling me sleep, all I felt was pain. I grimaced and tried to break free, but I couldn't get past the throbbing in my head. "It is true that I want her by my side, but she is not a necessity."

"She's your daughter…"

"Kain!" I yelled out. Not because he revealed what he knew, but because my breath had been ripped from my lungs. I felt like I was drowning. Searing waves of pain shot through every limb until I wanted to collapse and die.

"Stop it! Stop it!" Kain screamed at Lucian. I didn't know what he was doing to me, but it hurt like hell. "I won't do anything. Just don't kill her, please." For as much as Kain tried to be a stoic leader, his persona crumbled into pieces. Fresh tears glistened in his eyes as he pleaded for this to stop. He cared about me so much, and the little part of me not in agony understood how deep his love went.

"Good." Lucian said and all of my pain instantly went away. I sucked in a few gasping breaths of air, aware that there was nothing to cough out. Even though it felt like water, my lungs were clear.

"Let's go."

Lucian pushed me out the door, and I had one last chance to look at the puddles that used to be Abhainn and then back to Kain before the door closed shut. Lucian had hurt so many of my friends and family, and now it appeared that he was going to hurt more.

I had no choice but to obey.

SIXTEEN

Kain

The second the door closed, I fought back. Graham was distracted by Lucian and Eviana's exit, and the pressure from his forearm pushing against my throat lightened enough for me to strike. I hit him as hard as I could in the side of his face with my left hand. It wasn't pretty, and Troy would probably laugh at me, but it worked. And when he let go of my throat to face me, I slammed my forehead into his nose. The move sent shock waves through my head.

"What the…" Graham said, holding his nose and taking two steps backward. "You son of a…" I kicked him in the stomach and watched him fall to the ground. In a split second, I was holding the traitor by the throat and getting ready to land another punch.

"I wouldn't do that if I were you," he managed to spit out past the blood in his mouth. "Something happens to me, she dies."

I froze. Did I chance it? What would one more hit do anyway? I swung my fist forward and enjoyed the sound of it making contact with his cheek. It wasn't like the noise in movies, more like the slapping of a wet towel against the floor. Not fancy but effective.

I felt my knuckles split with that last blow and shaking my hand, I lowered my face close to Graham's. "That was for Abhainn. And now you will help me out of this. Do you understand?"

He smiled. "Are you trying to persuade me or force me?" I looked down at him in confusion. "I can feel you pushing against my mind, but it won't work." What was he talking about? Merfolk couldn't use compulsion against each other.

My head suddenly throbbed, and the night Lucian stabbed me came flooding back into the forefront of my mind. Eviana and I had a physical reaction to Lucian's compulsion of the selkies. Something similar to what I was feeling now.

Without a conscious thought, I sat down on the floor, off to the side of Graham. There was an overwhelming urge to sleep. Why was I so tired? Graham pushed himself up and grabbed a paper towel. After running it under the faucet, he wiped the blood off his face while keeping an eye on me.

"You don't stand a chance, bloke. One wrong move and you'll die or she'll die." He shrugged his shoulders. "I'd prefer it if you disappeared since I am very much looking forward to spending my nights alone with her. She is a feisty tart. It will certainly make for an interesting marriage." And then he had the nerve to wink at me.

Whatever hold he had over me at that point shattered into a thousand pieces. Graham was a pompous ass, a powerful Council member, and an all around jerk. But I think it was the idea that I could lose Eviana to yet another guy who didn't deserve her. Not again. I wouldn't sit back and let that happen this time.

I threw out my hand and commanded the water still falling from the faucet to lift up into the air and wrap around Graham's throat. Caught off guard, he dropped the towel and pulled against the strands. His fingers passed through to no avail. The mix of water and blood made for a horrid site. I felt an evil sense of satisfaction I didn't know I possessed.

Forcing the water to squeeze tighter, Graham's eyes widened just before a smile passed over his face. He wrinkled his forehead and glared at me. A piercing pain sliced through my head, causing me to lose my concentration.

"You can't beat me," he spat. With his accent, it sounded less like a threat and more like a royal reprimand. It made me laugh. Until he forced me to walk toward him.

"How are you doing this?" I asked. Apparently he wasn't able to control my thoughts completely.

"I'm gifted," he replied. "And you…you will remember that the next time you try one of your little stunts." He reached out and punched me so hard in the stomach that it brought tears to my eyes. I made a move toward him and got shoved back into the wall in response.

"Enough of this. I tire of your games." Graham's hands wrapped around my throat tight enough that I couldn't breathe. "Make one more attempt you ignorant syrenka, and I will kill her myself." Something in his demeanor had changed. For the first time tonight, I believed in his threat.

Holding my hands out to the side, I signaled my surrender. Fighting Graham would only get Eviana killed. We needed to know what Lucian's game was, and being stuck in this bathroom with a guy I hated would not get us anywhere. Eviana was out there, doing her part. It was time for me to do the same.

Seeing my resolution, Graham stepped away and picked the towel up off the floor. "Make yourself presentable. I may tolerate your actions, but Lucian certainly won't. If he sees us like this, he will do something horrible to you." Then he looked at me, deep in thought. "No, he'll hurt her and make you watch. It's a thing of his."

"Why are you going along with this? I thought you cared about her?" I don't even know why I said it. I certainly didn't want to discuss this with him, but it I had to ask.

He continued wiping his face, using the mirror to find every last blood speck. "This is the way it has to be. We are too powerful to sit by and watch humans destroy everything. Besides, Eviana will come around. She will see the light."

It took everything I had, mostly my loyalty to Eviana and my clan, to stand still and listen to his nonsense. I kept telling myself that I'd have my chance to get even with him, I just had to bide my time.

Without another incident, I followed him out of the restroom and into the meeting area. When we got close enough for people to notice us, Graham slowed so that he moved behind me.

"Don't even think about trying anything." He pushed my shoulder forward, turning me so that I could see Eviana and Lucian standing on the far side of the room. Her eyes searched frantically through the crowd until she spotted me. We exchanged another knowing look that sent my heart into a free fall. I couldn't let him take her from me.

"Ain't love grand?" Graham whispered behind me. I shot him a look that went unanswered. Instead he chuckled and pushed me further into the room and toward the closest wall. There were several rows of chairs facing one direction with a center aisle that led to a lone microphone in the front of the room. A perfect way to demand attention from all.

My only other ally in this meeting was Adele. As the leader of the American Council, she was devastated to hear about Graham's betrayal. She had taken him under her wing when his parents couldn't manage him and his powers anymore. Together they worked to control and master his skills, only to have him use them against his own kind. I will never forget the look on her face the moment it all sunk in. Disappointment of that magnitude was hard to overcome.

As if on cue, the American Council, with their maroon cloaks and solemn faces, made their way to the chairs in the front row. Or at least some of them did. I counted only four moving to the left side, while two others broke to the right. The seventh one was playing guard duty next to me.

"Won't they suspect something if you aren't with them?" I asked in a whisper.

"They already know," he said. Something about his tone worried me, but I was distracted by the screech of a microphone.

"Sit," Lucian commanded from his new position behind the microphone. The right side of the room obeyed instantly, including Eviana. Although she moved stiffly and I swear I saw tears in her eyes. I would kill him for putting her through this.

The left side of the room, a mixture of cloaks representing Council's from all over the world, hesitated. I caught Adele staring behind me at Graham. If she would have been able to compel with her look, Graham would have been dead. Instead he smiled at her and bent forward in a mock bow. Without thinking, I elbowed him hard in the ribs, and then resumed my stance so as to not attract attention.

Eviana jumped to her feet, obviously watching the exchange. Graham recovered quickly and in retaliation, he forced himself into my mind. I was frozen, stuck to the floor like a concrete statue. I hated that he could do this.

"You try that again and I will show you the extent of my power," he threatened.

I wanted to reply with something witty or sarcastic, but I couldn't speak. If I got out of here, I needed to work on my compulsion. On merfolk.

Lucian's eyes flashed in our direction and I felt Graham stiffen behind me. In just a few seconds, Lucian had control of the room and our little scuffle was getting too loud. Graham released his mental hold on me, but placed one hand on my shoulder as a reminder of his presence. We were both conveniently facing Eviana, and I knew that wasn't a coincidence. I had to behave for her sake.

She finally sat back down. A look passed over Lucian's face that I couldn't interpret as he watched her succumb like the rest of the merfolk in the room.

"I must thank you all for coming on such short notice," Lucian began. I finally took in the atmosphere. There must have been at least fifty powerful Council members here, somewhat equally divided between the two sides of the room. I feared this division had a greater meaning.

"As a courtesy, I will get right to the point," Lucian continued. "It is time for our kind to take back what is ours. No more hiding behind humans and watching them destroy our heritage. For too long they have been allowed to believe that they rule over all, and for too long we have stayed in the shadows and let this atrocity unfold." He spread his arms out wide and turned to face the left side of the room.

"I blame you for their arrogance and ignorance. Your unwillingness to keep them in line has led to war, famine, and overpopulation. They are slowly killing us. All of us. The sprites, the nymphs, the ratchets…we are all suffering because of your incompetence." He turned back to the other side of the room which I now realized contained his supporters. It was where Eviana sat, along with two of the American Council members. Adele and Christopher. My stomach dropped. What did he threaten Adele with? It must have been horrible for her to be a part of this charade.

"We have decided that it is time for a new leadership to guide us toward The Legacy. No longer will we be weakened by those too scared to act. Effectively immediately, there will be *one* united Council comprised of eight members chosen by me and supported by all of you."

I watched the crowd closely. Most were looking at him in awe, but some showed fear and wariness. Unfortunately, one of them decided to speak.

"You do not have the privilege of making those demands, Lucian." It was an older man, ancient really. His Spanish accent and black cloak lead me to believe that he represented one of the South American Councils.

"My old friend, Gabriel. How you have been mislead. I can make these demands and you all *will* listen to me."

Without uttering a sound, Lucian focused on Gabriel. The ancient leader gasped for air and clutched at his heart. Those seated around him jumped up and cleared a space encircling the ailing merman like a noose. Lucian smiled until Adele stood. He gave her one look, so menacing and wicked, that she stopped herself from doing anything more.

Gabriel took one last painful breath that squeaked more than it should, before collapsing to the ground. He never moved again.

"What did you do?" Another mermaid with a gold cloak screamed at Lucian. She appeared to be more afraid than angry.

"I did what we all should be doing. I controlled him." A chorus of gasps and whispers made their way through the room. The sheer panic written on the faces of those who'd sided against Lucian was evident.

"How?" someone yelled.

"It is my legacy, fools. You've heard the stories since you were children. My family has always held enhanced powers of compulsion, but you were all too ignorant to accept this."

It was almost as if I could see each person digging through their minds. I remembered the stories told at parties to scare the younger merfolk. Stories about those like us who had the ability to kill you with one look. Those who had the ability to compel other merfolk. Like Graham and Lucian. And maybe like me.

"This is the way it should be. Survival of the fittest. And a new pecking order will be established today." Lucian motioned to one of his selkie guards who promptly joined him by the microphone. "I have already taken the first steps in conquering this new world of ours." The selkie handed him an electronic device with a small screen. Lucian turned it toward the audience and pointed to a map. "I have found that humans from this part of the world are particularly favorable of war, even without compulsion. With a little push from me and my colleagues, we have created a situation where a nuclear attack is eminent. One suggestion, one *push* from us and millions of humans will die." He actually smiled while the merfolk shifted in their seats. "Humans are weak. A flood, famine, disease, war…it won't take much to rid us of these overpopulated rats."

Lucian handed the device back to the selkie and held up his hands. "However, we don't have to resort to extreme violence and death right away. We can utilize humans to do our bidding, to work for the merfolk. Many of us already have contacts in powerful positions, now is the time to make more. With changes in policy and the quick destruction of those who get in our way, the world will be back under our control in no time." He paused dramatically.

"I will lead you all in this endeavor, but I will not do it alone," Lucian continued, his tone daring someone to challenge him. "My daughter will rule by my side." He lifted his arm during the chorus of whispers, beckoning Eviana to come stand beside him.

I saw her hesitation, as did Lucian. He jerked his head in my direction forcing Eviana to look at me. At the same time Graham squeezed the back of my neck, and once again I struggled against the urge to fight back.

She mouthed the words "I'm sorry" to me and shuffled to Lucian's side. I shrugged off Graham's hand and took a step in her direction, but was cut off by Lucian's next words.

"There are six more of you chosen ones that will accompany us in this new world. Christopher Walters, please stand."

The Council member who'd always seemed partial to Lucian's behavior, stood with smirk on his face that made me want to punch him.

"Elizabetta Morganti." A middle aged female in a gold cloak stood while the rest of the Council members around her made little attempt to hide their disgust. Her dark hair flowed down the back of her cloak like silk and her confident stance let everyone know how honored she was. The look she gave Lucian, like he was the only man in the room, had me wondering about the extent of their relationship, and then immediately trying to scratch it from my mind.

"Dominique Bené, Petra Zukov, and Peder Borja, I welcome you to my side." Three more Council members from the Caribbean

Nations, Eastern Europe, and Scandinavian factions walked to the front of the room, oblivious to the hateful glares they received from their fellow leaders.

That made seven, until I heard Graham shift behind me. "And last, but certainly not least, Graham Forrester," Lucian bellowed.

All fifty heads turned to the merman still standing beside me with his hand on my shoulder. I saw Graham nod out of the corner of my eye and Lucian actually smiled. It was a real smile too, like a public display of a father's pride. I feared we'd greatly underestimated the dynamic between the two of them.

"Graham Forrester is not only a very powerful merman and leader of our kind, but he will soon be my son-in-law." Eviana hung her head and my heart stopped. It was bittersweet. On one hand I knew she hated to be forced into marriage, and on the other, I'd been the one she'd refused in the past.

"My beautiful daughter will be married in two days, securing the future of our beliefs and the abilities that should be celebrated not feared." Members of the newly formed Council clapped their hands together, as did the entire right side of the room. It reminded me of human political speeches where the supporters stood and clapped at every word uttered by their party leader.

"To honor this occasion, I will be holding our first official meeting in the same evening, and I expect you all to attend." He glared at the left side of the room. "Your presence is required. As representatives of our kind, you owe it to your people to understand how things will be done from now on."

I watched in awe as not a single one of them argued with the insanity behind what Lucian was asking them to do. They simply sat there...like zombies. Could he control that many merfolk at once?

"Adele Lyonetta will provide you with the location and details. We will celebrate the birth of a new union and a new way of life." I swear his teeth glimmered in the light. Half of the room erupted in cheers while the other half sat silent and still. I wondered if they would really follow through with Lucian's idiotic demands.

"You will have a front row seat, mate." Graham slapped me hard against the back and I gritted my teeth together.

"Get your hand off me," I growled.

"Now, now," he continued patting my back. "There are plenty of fish in the sea for someone like you. Don't be a sore loser."

I turned to face him and he shook a finger in my face. "Don't even think about it. I may be more than willing to marry her, but it would give me greater pleasure to see you suffer."

I couldn't think. In one breath, Graham threatened to both enjoy Eviana in ways only a husband should and kill her at the same time to spite me. At that moment I knew that I would do anything to stop this. But now wasn't the time.

Lucian walked down the center pathway between the chairs, pulling Eviana behind. She wasn't putting up too much of a fight, but it was obvious to me that she also wasn't a willing participant. The rest of his newfound Council glided behind him like they'd just won a pageant.

"Time for me to go chump," Graham said, drawing my attention away from Eviana. "I will see you at the wedding. Be sure to dress nice."

I hated his stupid accent and his cocky face. I glared at the back of his head while he joined the others and thought of a thousand ways to take him out.

My eyes caught Adele's and without saying a word, I knew that we were thinking the same thing. We had two days to figure out a way to finish this.

Two days.

SEVENTEEN

Eviana

The return flight to Lucian's home wasn't exactly what I was expecting. We never went back to Mexico, instead we landed on a small sandy runway in the outskirts of the Bahamas. Exhaustion overruled my normal fear of airplanes this trip. It was two in the morning, and I hardly felt like dealing with Lucian's antics. Nor did I want to deal with my annoying British fiancé.

"Wasn't that so exciting, tart?" Graham asked me for at least the hundredth time. "The look on their faces…they didn't know what was coming."

His excitement over Lucian's new Council and the betrayal of so many merfolk made me sick. Even worse, I had a lot of time to think about Abhainn and Kain. I'd never seen someone force a sprite to disintegrate and I really feared Lucian had killed him. After being trapped in a fountain for so many years, this was not the death

Abhainn deserved. He should have been able to grow old and die peacefully next to the love of his life. Thinking about Isabel, I wondered how well she would handle the news. I'd bet that Lucian just acquired a new enemy.

Kain's face haunted my visions as well. I could see the wheels turning in his brain when we exchanged a look during the meeting. He wouldn't give up on me, but I certainly didn't want him to die. A life spent in agony with Graham and Lucian was better than one where I knew Kain had died senselessly.

"When are we going to meet with her?" Graham asked Lucian as we climbed down the airplane stairs and into the blistering humidity of the dark evening.

"Tomorrow," he said and then looked at me. "We don't have much time to prepare. She has to be ready tomorrow."

"I'm standing right here," I said, annoyed that they were speaking about me as though I was an inanimate object. "Who am I going to meet and why do I have to do that?" Each minute felt like I was biding my time until the wedding. Surely someone would have a plan that involved defeating Lucian, right? There is no way that merfolk would sit back and let him rule. That wasn't an option.

But even as I thought those words, I deep pit of worry dredge in my stomach and I feared the worst. Lucian had been smart this time. He gave power to others, effectively solidifying his support. Half of the leaders in the meeting had already expressed their beliefs in his strategy, and all they had to do was command their clans to listen. I suddenly realized this might be the end of the battle, and my legs almost collapsed underneath me.

Graham reached out and caught my waist before I hit the ground. "Whoa there, luv. Are you okay?"

I pushed away from him, angry with my body for feeling a wave of excitement from his touch. "Get away. I'm fine." Graham looked genuinely hurt, but Lucian smirked and shook his head.

"I believe our Eviana has finally accepted her fate." He stepped closer to me and leaned into my face. "No one is going to save you now."

Swallowing a lump of fear stuck in my throat, I tried not to react to his threat. "Who am I going to see tomorrow?"

"It's a surprise," he hissed and stomped away from me. "Let's go, I'm tired." Lucian walked to the awaiting town car and climbed into the back seat. The car seemed a bit too fancy for the island surroundings, but that was by far the least of my concerns right now.

Graham held open the door for me, so I walked around him without saying a word and opened the front passenger door. Sliding in next to the stunned driver, I smiled. "Can I ride up here with you?"

The dimples in his cheeks divulged how young he was. "I would be honored," he replied.

Graham huffed as he climbed into the back and I purposely avoided looking into the mirror so I didn't have to see his face. We drove in silence for twenty minutes down a lone road paralleling the sea on both sides.

"Where are we?" I asked the driver. His eyes flickered to the rearview mirror, presumably waiting to see if any of my companions would answer. When no one responded, he shrugged his shoulders.

"Long Island, miss."

Long Island in the Bahamas. I didn't know much about it, but from what I could tell, there didn't seem to be a lot of people living here. We hadn't passed a street light since the airport, and aside from a few piles of concrete blocks, there wasn't a house in sight.

The car turned right just as the road ended in front of us. We were on the very tip of the island, far away from anyone or anything else. It was another perfect Lucian compound. The house sat atop a small hill with a full view of the ocean. It wasn't a large home, but the seclusion made up for the lack of space.

"We begin at sunrise tomorrow," Lucian said. He'd already entered the house, expecting everyone to follow. "There are three bedrooms, but sleep where you like."

For a second, I was taken aback by Lucian's casual suggestion that Graham and I could share a bed. Then I realized he probably did that just to get under my skin. He knew I wouldn't be spending any alone time with Graham. Ever.

As Lucian disappeared upstairs, the driver set our small bags just inside the door and turned to leave. "Wait! What's your name?" I asked him.

He looked startled at the question, as if no one had ever asked him that before. "My name is Robert, but everyone here calls me Lucky." He smiled and the dimples grew.

"Thank you, Lucky. I'm Eviana." I reached out to shake his hand, and he jumped when the screen door slammed shut behind me. It reminded me of the way an abused animal reacts to loud noises. Then again, he was a human working for Lucian. He probably had been abused.

Gently touching my hand, he squeezed it and nodded. "You be careful Miss Eviana."

"It's Mistress to you," Graham cut in. Lucky's grip tightened for an instant and then he walked backward toward the car.

"Mistress Eviana," he bowed his head slightly. "You let me know if there is anything you need. No matter what time it is."

"We are finished with your services. Good night." Graham's condescending tone made me angry. As I turned to say something to him, he interrupted me. "He's a human, Eviana. You don't need to be nice to him."

There were so many things I wanted to say, but I decided that the silent treatment would be much more effective. Pushing past him, I opened the screen door and picked up my bag. There wasn't much in it. Lucian said that there would be clothes for me here. I dreaded what he picked out for me.

I found the first bedroom down the hall and decided to claim it. As soon as I put my bag down, I heard Graham shuffling by the door.

"This will do," he said, eyeing up the bed. "Although I think there's a queen in the other room."

"You are not staying in here with me." He smiled, and a flood of memories from Jeremiah's house came swarming back into my mind. The way we flirted with each other, the workout sessions, the almost kiss. My heart pounded in my chest, and I hated it.

I hated that our blood was so attracted to each other when his presence alone should have repulsed me. For all of the lies and wickedness inside of him, he didn't make for a good catch. But his beautiful face and our natural attraction betrayed me.

"What's the problem? In two nights, you will be my wife. We could start the honeymoon early." He stepped a little too close so I kicked him between the legs right where I was aiming.

Graham yelled and doubled over in pain. His hands covered over the injured area as he fell to his knees. "You bitch! You will pay for this!"

I probably should have been scared, but his voice was high and squeaky and some evil part in me enjoyed his torment. "And you will never have me!" I pushed him backward and out the door, slamming it in his face before he had a chance to protest. There was a lock on the knob which I quickly turned, hoping that it would give me at least some protection. Although by the sound of Graham's moans, I didn't think I had anything to worry about.

Eventually I heard him slink away down the hall, mumbling curses the entire time. I probably should be sure to avoid any alone time with him tomorrow. He was definitely upset.

Yet when I woke early the next morning and found Lucian and Graham drinking coffee in the kitchen, he acted like our exchange never happened.

"Morning, luv. Coffee?" He pushed a large mug into my hands and bent forward to kiss my cheek. Unfortunately, I couldn't pull away fast enough.

"Did you two have a fun evening?" Lucian asked. The question was creepy for so many reasons. First of all, a father should be more protective of his daughter's virtue. And second, why would I ever discuss my personal sex life with him? And why would he want to know about it? I shivered in disgust but Graham was the one to answer.

"Eviana told me she wants our wedding night to be special, so I decided to honor that." He sipped his coffee and wiggled his eyebrows at me. I almost tossed the scalding liquid at his face. In fact, I don't really know why I restrained myself, except that it meant I had one more night alone.

"That is an honorable notion," Lucian said, and the two men clinked their mugs together in a toast. It was nauseating.

"Where are we going?" I asked.

"To see Amathia," Lucian said as though I should know who that was.

Graham's face lit up. "You will love her." I looked at him in confusion. "She's going to help you find your way."

"Stop speaking in riddles." Turning to Lucian, I added, "Who is she?"

"She is a nereid."

"A what?" I asked.

Lucian sighed. He dumped his coffee into the sink and rinsed his mug before answering me. "I could just kill your mother."

"You did!" I spat.

"Oh right. Yes, I did." My gut squeezed with sadness. How could he be so nonchalant about breaking her neck? "She really didn't teach you very well."

"She's a sea nymph," Graham said. For a moment I thought he was referring to my mother. Trying to get my heartbreak under control, I focused on his annoyingly handsome face.

"Like a naiad?" I asked.

"Yes, only nereid's live in saltwater." Graham looked at me with an intensity I didn't like. "You know about naiad's?"

"I've met one."

"Where?" Lucian asked. He seemed to be genuinely surprised.

"In Tennessee." With Brendan. He'd surprised me with a late night swim in a mountain lake that his dad had spoken about. We discovered the naiad, or really she discovered us, and it was the first time I learned that water nymphs weren't extinct as we had been taught. I felt my throat tighten up at the memories of that night in the lodge. It was the first time Brendan and I slept together. It was my eighteenth birthday and I thought we were going to spend the rest of our lives together away from all of the drama that came along with being who we were.

I couldn't have been more wrong.

"Now that is fascinating. I haven't seen a naiad since I was a boy." Lucian tapped his chin. "You must take me to meet that one someday." I stayed silent, not wanting to commit to anything in the future that involved Lucian.

"Let's go. We don't want to keep Amathia waiting." Lucian ushered us to the door and outside toward the car. Lucky was leaning against the side, staring out at the sea. Even though he wore a dark suit, he didn't appear to be sweating and I wondered how he could stand the heat.

"Good morning, Mistress Eviana," he said with a smile.

"Good morning, Lucky" I replied being sure to let Graham see me. He rolled his eyes and didn't say anything when I climbed into the front passenger seat again. Good.

"Take us to Dean's Blue Hole," Lucian ordered from the back seat. Lucky looked alarmed.

"Master Sutherland, there will be a crowd there today." I snapped my head around, surprised that Lucky seemed to know we weren't human. He didn't appear to be under Lucian's influence, yet he *chose* to work for him. I found myself reassessing my opinion of the man.

"That's not of my concern," Lucian said.

The car lurched forward and down the tiny hill to the only road to and from this part of the island. I'd forgotten how much I loved the clear blues and greens of the tropics. Sure, California had a beautiful underwater landscape, but nothing compared to the inviting nature of the shallow, sloping east coast.

We passed through a town where I assumed the majority of the population resided. Colorful plywood stores, interspersed with unfinished concrete homes, decorated the streets. Dogs and children played in the road, waving to us as we drove by. Within a few minutes, we passed through the metropolis and were surrounded by mangroves and limestone again.

"Stop here," Lucian commanded a few minutes later. Lucky slammed on his brakes and I had to brace myself against the dash board.

"But sir, the hole is still a mile away." Lucky was speaking to air since Lucian had already opened his door and jumped out of the car. Graham and I followed.

"Come back for us at sunset," Lucian yelled to Lucky, who nodded and drove away.

"Sunset?" Graham asked, taking the words right out of my mouth.

Lucian looked at me. In my little sundress, I felt exposed under his stare. "She will need all day with her." Suddenly, I wasn't so excited to meet this nereid.

"We will swim there so that I can take care of the tourists." Lucian started to strip out of his clothes.

"What do you mean 'take care of'," I asked.

He smiled and shook his head. "They're going to think the water is too murky for a swim, Eviana. I'm not going to kill them."

"Well, that's a surprise," I said sarcastically.

"You will soon learn that we aren't really that horrible," Graham cut in. When I turned my head to face him, I couldn't stop the heat from rising to my cheeks. He was completely naked and not making any attempt at modesty. His stomach muscles were undeniably perfect where they connected to his lower abdomen. I cursed my body again for its reaction. "Here, let me help you with that." Graham grabbed the strap of my dress.

I slapped his hand away. "I've got it," I growled.

"Come now, children," Lucian said. He walked down a barely there sandy pathway, that flowed over and around large chunks of limestone rocks and sand nettles. Folding his clothes into a neat little pile, Lucian tucked them between the stems of a mangrove and sauntered into the ocean. As soon as he was waist deep, he disappeared under the surface.

"Are you sure you don't need any help, tart?" Graham laughed at my glare then proceeded to shake his rear end in ways that insinuated so much, I had to look away. I wondered if a blood transfusion would get rid of this attraction between us.

Suddenly I noticed that I was alone. Perhaps I could run away. But where would I go? There was no way off of this island without having some help. I wanted to leave, but I didn't want Lucian to kill Kain. Plus, I will admit that I was curious to see this nereid and find out what she was supposed to help me with.

Deciding to go along with the plan, I dove into the water and felt the quick transition into my other form. My hand brushed against my hip, searching for my double wave clan pendant. I hadn't had it since Lucian took it away before his meeting, and I missed it greatly. Although, I was surprised that my transformation was smooth, considering I didn't have the power of being a clan leader attached to me anymore. Something seemed to be changing in me.

I caught up with the two of them a few hundred yards offshore. Graham waited for me with an outstretched arm. I ignored the invitation to play handsies with him and swam closer to Lucian. Graham pulled on my tail, trying to get my attention. I kicked at him hard and almost gave him a bloody nose.

In less than ten minutes, we swam around a rock outcropping into a protected cove. I could see the deep blue water of the hole ahead of us, but we stopped and surfaced before reaching it.

"What are we..." I started to ask but Lucian hushed me. I followed his gaze toward the shore and saw a handful of humans preparing their SCUBA tanks and snorkeling gear. Lucian's forehead wrinkled in concentration. I watched a few of the humans stand and walk to the water's edge. I really hoped Lucian wasn't going to make them drown.

But I breathed a sigh of relief when they bent forward to test the water and then shook their heads. I heard one of them tell the others to gather their gear because the conditions were not going to be good for visibility. Looking disappointed, the rest of them complied. Within a few minutes, the beach was clear. The last of the divers placed a flag in the sand, presumably indicating that the hole was closed for the day.

That's because we had a nereid to meet.

"Come, she is expecting us," Lucian said before diving below the surface again. We swam into the middle of the hole and waited. The giant cavern was so deep that I couldn't see the bottom, even with my enhanced mermaid vision. But the sheer beauty of the place set my mind at peace.

All around us sunlight filtered through the surface, refracting in an unnatural way. The dark interspersed with the light, created shadows that had me thinking I was seeing things.

Lucian tapped me on the shoulder and pointed down below us into the abyss. At first, I didn't notice it. A trail of tiny bubbles rose up to the surface in front of our eyes, but Lucian was looking at the source below.

And when I saw it, I nearly screamed.

EIGHTEEN

Eviana

I noticed the teeth first. Sharp, white fangs larger than a ratchet's rose up from the depths at an incredible speed. Her face contorted into a horrific form, snarling and wrinkled and deadly.

The bubble tornado spiraled past us and shot to the surface. In its wake I could see tendrils of hair and something else. It looked like jellyfish tentacles, and just as I was trying to get a closer look, Lucian yanked me back out of the way. He shook his head, warning me to stay back, and then pulled me up to the surface.

When we broke through the water, I immediately wanted to ask him what was happening, but the sight in front of me rendered me speechless. The nereid, terrifying and hideous below the surface, now reminded me of a sea goddess. Her delicate form floated gracefully across the water. The tentacles had transformed into a silver flowing dress, although when I looked closer, I could still see the life in it.

Each strand moved as though it had a mind of its own. Similar to the dress, her long blonde hair wavered in the air like extensions of her arms. I remembered the lake naiad using her hair to touch Brendan and me, and a wave of chills swept through my body.

Amathia's head snapped in my direction, her hair and dress tentacles following a few seconds later. "You have seen one of us before?" Her whisper-like voice echoed in the air. It was so beautiful and soothing, I could only nod in response. I knew she would be able to read my thoughts like the other sprites.

"Amathia, it has been too long." Lucian captured the nereid's attention. She studied him for a moment and then swept across the surface to come closer. Sinking into the water so that she was at eye level with us, her hair began to caress Lucian's face. His eyes closed and he smiled.

Amathia continued to touch Lucian's face, neck, and shoulders. Graham watched with an expression that was very close to being star stuck. I thought that it was such an intimate moment, I almost looked away.

"You need something from me," she stated. There was a slight accent to her voice. Something ancient and wise.

"Yes. We need your help," Lucian answered, eyes still closed seeming to enjoy the nereid's touch.

"Yes. Yes, you do. It has been a while since I've been asked to awaken one of you." She rose to the surface again and turned to look at Graham. A piece of her tentacle dress reached out and wrapped around his head. I watched his mouth curl into a blissful smile as his eyes stared at Amathia's beautiful face. "I shall enjoy teaching this one."

I swear I saw her appearance change ever so slightly so that she now looked ten years younger; closer to my age. Her focus on Graham intensified as she continued to alter her image.

"You are young. And now I am young for you." She bent forward and kissed Graham on the mouth. It wasn't an innocent kiss either and after a few seconds, Lucian stopped her.

"Amathia, my daughter needs you. Not Graham." She recoiled so quickly that her hair practically pulled Graham with her.

"A female?" Something about her tone sped up my heartbeat. Her face flashed back to the creature we first saw below the surface. It was only for an instant, but it scared me. "I haven't had a female for centuries."

I certainly didn't like the sound of that, but Lucian seemed unconcerned. "My daughter has the blood of leaders in her, but she has been untrained by those who raised her. I have prepared her for you the best I could, but it is time for the awakening."

"You *prepared* me?" I asked before I could stop myself. "The drugs?"

Lucian nodded to me and then looked back at the nereid. "She will fulfill our destiny."

"The Legacy?" Amathia asked but it wasn't kind. "You want me to awaken her so that she can control me too?"

Lucian swam a little closer to her. "Amathia, you are a goddess of your kind. Powerful, beautiful, seductive. You cannot be controlled. Ever." If I didn't know any better, I'd say Lucian was flirting with her.

"I *am* a goddess, Lucian Sutherland. And it would be wise for you to remember that." Her hair reached out toward Lucian and started to caress his face again. But then he jerked back in surprise and she lifted one of the tendrils to her mouth. Lucian rubbed his neck and when he pulled his hand away, I noticed the blood. Amathia suckled on the tip of the tendril, enjoying the taste of Lucian. "Delightful. And powerful." Her body shivered in satisfaction.

I didn't want to be here any longer.

"Will you help her?" Lucian finally asked, his flirtatious tone no longer in his voice.

Two tentacles from her dress reached out and grabbed me so quickly that I didn't have time to react. She pulled me to her at the same time she lowered herself to my level. Her hands and tendrils ran through my hair and stroked my face. A wave of calm washed over me and I understood why the guys had been so content under her touch. It was as though nothing else in the world mattered. It was peaceful.

Somewhere in the back of my mind I could hear them talking. "I can feel it in her," Amathia was saying.

"Yes, she will far surpass me in time," Lucian answered. He sounded proud.

"I will need the day," Amathia said, eyes never leaving mine. "And a taste of that one."

"Agreed," Lucian said. I assumed she wanted to taste Graham, but I was too enthralled to realize how disturbing that was. Until I saw her face change.

Her eyes turned black and soulless. Her mouth widened to an unnatural size. And the fangs reappeared. "This will only hurt for a moment," she said just before opening her mouth and biting down into the side of my neck.

I tried to scream, but the pain racing through my neck was too intense. Amathia's bite never faltered and I could feel her fangs burying deeper and deeper into my flesh. I feared she was going to bite clear through.

We spiraled down into the depths of the hole in a free fall. I barely noticed the blues of the shallows disappear into the blackness hundreds of feet below. Amathia began to make a noise that pierced through my ears. It sounded like a falcon dying a horrible death. Her screams continued until we slammed against the bottom of the hole. It was dark and cold, and I knew that I was going to die down here.

You will live. Amathia's voice pushed into my mind, which did not have a calming effect. How was she doing that? My chest burned with its need for more oxygen. Diving this deep was not impossible for us, but the pressure limited our air capacity.

I began to panic. Lucian made this happen. He was trying to kill me, I just knew it. I used what little air I had left getting upset over Lucian's betrayal, and prepared myself to drown. It's not an easy feat; accepting that death is a few seconds away. Deciding to give up. It's not really what I wanted, but there was a nereid holding me six hundred feet below the sea, drinking my blood and denying me oxygen. Death seemed like the obvious conclusion.

You will live, Amathia said again and I think I chuckled at that sentiment. There was no way I could make it through this. As that thought filtered through my mind, Amathia pulled her fangs out of my neck and covered my mouth with hers.

She kissed me. But it wasn't like a regular kiss. It was like her mouth was a passageway to the surface. My lungs filled with oxygen, and a euphoric sense of peace washed over me. *Let me in*, she said. Although consciously, I didn't know what she meant, I felt my body relax and let her presence fill me. In an instant, everything went black.

I woke up with a shock and sucked in a huge breath. But something was wrong. Where was I? What just happened? My brain moved through a fog as it tried to process the situation. I was sitting in the dark on the bottom of the ocean. The blue hole. I remembered that I was in an ancient sinkhole, but I shouldn't be *breathing*.

I was in my mermaid form, yet I felt different. Stronger. I sucked in another breath and didn't cough or sputter or drown like I should have. It was exhilarating.

A dark shadow darted past me. Then another, and another. I was suddenly surrounded by creatures too dark to see clearly, but similar in size as me. They began to shriek while swimming in a circle around me. I covered my ears to block the awful sound, willing them stop. When that didn't work, I threw my hands out toward them trying to use the water as a weapon.

It worked. Wisps of seawater sprang out of my hands and wrapped around the black bodies of the shadow creatures. They screamed and screeched as, one by one, they shattered into pieces. I didn't fully understand what was happening, but I had to smile. I'd just used water control in the same way Kain and Graham did. Now if I could figure out how to get out of here, I would be a very happy girl.

When I tried to move, I started to lose hope. It was like I was stuck to the ground, unable to lift anything except my arms. I took another breath. Weird. I couldn't swim, but I could breathe. I couldn't force my tail off the ground, but I could suddenly control the water better than ever. I didn't understand.

You are awakening. It was a strange echo of a voice that instantly soothed my mind. *Give in to it and you shall thrive.*

Give in to it? It didn't seem like I had enough control over my body to give it commands. I tried to swim again to no avail. How was I supposed to go through with this?

In a flash, something slammed into my chest. I fell backward so that I was lying completely on the bottom, looking up at the surface where I hoped someone was waiting for me. I felt several tiny feet walking along my body from my tail and moving up toward my chest. My head was paralyzed, as well as my arms. The only thing moving now was my racing heart.

One slow step at a time, the thing on top of me inched closer to my face. I still couldn't see what it was, but the little feet felt like daggers digging into my skin. One by one, they crawled up my stomach, my chest, until finally stopping.

Amathia's face frightened me to the core. Her head was no longer shaped like a human, but more like the water sprites I'd encountered at Jeremiah's pool. Oblong things with slanted eyes and hundreds of pointed teeth. She hissed at me at the same time her hair sprawled out from her head like a cobra preparing to strike. And I couldn't move.

Let me in, she whispered. I tried to shake my head. Amathia lowered her mouth inches from my skin and proceeded to lick my neck and face in one long movement. Her tongue split down the center and was longer than any snake I'd ever seen before.

Let me in! This time I could hear the command in her voice and another round of fear fluttered in my stomach. Yet for some reason, I shook my head in denial again.

Amathia, the nereid of the sea, threw her head back and screamed. It lasted for minutes, maybe hours, I couldn't tell. But I do know that it was horrendous. My ears felt like they would bleed in response to her shrill cry. When she finally stopped, I sighed in relief. If I made it out of here, surely I would have some hearing damage.

Her tiny feet continued to climb closer to my face. How many feet did she have anyway? I squeezed my eyes shut, fearful of what she might look like now. Although imagining it in my head was probably worse than seeing it for myself.

Open your eyes, Eviana. And unlike the rest of her commands, I couldn't fight it. My eyes opened on their own to focus on her beautiful human face. She'd changed her appearance again. I was enchanted by her eyes and the sense of peace they brought to me. I stared at her willingly, not wanting it to end.

Amathia's hair flowed around her head like a crown. The tentacles from her dress rubbed my arms and tail, sending shivers through my skin. I thought she was going to kiss me again when she lowered her face next to mine. And I *wanted* her to kiss me. I wanted her breath, her power. I wanted to let her in.

Now! She yelled in my mind and I saw a bright flash of white before a stabbing pain penetrated my skull. In seconds, everything and everyone in my life flashed in front of me. Brendan at our sanctuary, Marisol and I playing in the water with my parents, watching Kain leave my house the night before our wedding. I saw glimpses of Palmer, Graham, Troy, Abhainn, and Isabel. Some of the images ripped from my memories and some of them created by Amathia.

There was a war. A battle in the sea between merfolk. I couldn't see faces, but I *felt* those I loved being harmed. In the center of the fight, I stood still. Watching. Waiting. For what, I didn't know. I was simply an observer seeing the depths to which merfolk would go to defend their beliefs.

Was this the future? Was this happening now? How long had I been trapped in this hole? A thousand questions flitted through my mind as I watched merfolk, selkies, and sprites die in battle. I tried to move, tried to fight. I needed to do something.

At once, a wall of water encircled me and I saw Amathia's face. She held two long, silver swords in her hands and she looked at me like I was a tasty morsel of sweet chocolate.

"What do you want?" I screamed at her, afraid of what was coming next. She simply smiled. Her fangs bit into her bottom lip, but she didn't notice. I watched several drops of dark blue blood fall from her mouth and disappear into the water below.

Off to the side, Kain cried out in pain. His face became clear and we looked at each other as a merman stood over him, ready to inflict the final blow with his knife.

Help him, Amathia's hollow voice echoed in my head.

I don't know how, I replied, somehow understanding she would hear me. In slow motion, the merman brought his knife down toward Kain's chest. I wanted to stop him. I needed to stop him. I pushed out with my mind in a last ditch effort.

And the merman stopped moving. He dropped the knife and fell to his knees. The sound of fighting ceased all around me and I was stunned to see everyone staring at me. Some had faces, some were just generic images of those I did not know, but they had all succumbed to my command.

Good, Amathia whispered, just before she plunged both swords into my stomach. Screaming in pain, I reached for the swords now penetrating my body. I tried to pull them out, but the nereid held them in place

"Why?" I asked in between sobs. "Why now?"

It is time for you to wake up. I didn't understand. I was awake, wasn't I?

Another burst of white light sent me back into the belly of the blue hole. Amathia's face lingered over top of mine and I could still feel the swords piercing my stomach. Surely I was going to die now.

Amathia smiled, revealing her true nature again, and thrust her fangs into my neck. I shouted out in fear, but no noise left my mouth. It didn't take long before I began to lose consciousness.

It felt like I was floating upward. The sky got brighter and the sides of the hole leapt out of the darkness. My arms dragged behind me like broken wings and I was unable to move my tail. The pain in my stomach was almost too much to bear, and I wished that I would pass out for good.

Someone grabbed me around the waist and propelled me closer to the surface. There was a part of me that knew I needed air, but despite what happened below, I didn't dare try to breathe under the water.

The warmth of the sun and the orange, pinks, and blues of the sky welcomed me at the surface. I took in a large gasp of air, and turned to the side just enough to see Lucian holding me in his arms.

"You're okay, Eviana. You did it," he whispered smoothly into my ear.

I couldn't fully comprehend what he was talking about, and the last thing I remembered was a bird flying over my head and off into the setting sun.

Nineteen

Kain

Before we left Lucian's meeting, Adele had a chance to pull me aside. Her frantic tone contradicted the determination in her voice. "We cannot let this happen. Let's meet tomorrow. I will contact you."

It was a rather cryptic message since we both knew that many eyes were watching. I didn't even have a chance to find out what Lucian had done to threaten her, but apparently she wasn't going to let that stop her completely.

Later that evening, I received a message that she would stop in California on her way home to Seattle, and we agreed to meet at Eviana's house. It practically felt like my home now as well, plus the selkie leader and some of our best protectors were still there. Surely they would want to hear what Adele had to say.

I informed Troy, Palmer, Malcolm, and Julian that the merfolk leaders would be coming today. I didn't know how many Adele was bringing with her, but hopefully she chose her friends wisely. The clans and Councils seemed to be equally divided in this war, so decisions couldn't be made in haste. A friend today could very well be an enemy tomorrow.

There was one person, or sprite, missing from the group. I hadn't seen Abhainn since Lucian shattered him at the meeting last night. Abhainn would often disappear that way on his own accord, but Lucian had forced it on him and I worried that wasn't good for his kind.

I made my way to the oceanfront in the few extra minutes I had before Adele's arrival. Hoping to see some sign of a water sprite, any water sprite, I scanned the horizon. It was a calm day in the sea and the sunlight reflected brightly enough to create a mirror effect. A shimmering wave caught my attention, and my stomach fluttered with excitement. Who would have thought, just a few months ago, that I'd be so happy to see a water sprite? In that short period of time, Abhainn and I had become great friends. He'd taught me so much about my water control abilities despite the fact it was his biggest fear about my kind. And his relationship with Isabel was inspiring. Two individuals from different backgrounds finding a way to make it work. It had given me hope.

The shadow of a wave I thought I saw disappeared and I feared that my eyes had played a trick on me. Knowing I had just a few minutes left, I started calling for him. It worked once before, so now I wished for the same result.

Again, I noticed something that looked like a head pop up and out of the water just a few yards offshore. I watched as that head expanded into a body and emerged from the breaking waves. Even with the sun glaring against the surface, I recognized Isabel's long hair and perfectly shaped human body. I guess if you can shift into any form, why not make it exceptional.

She was hunched forward dragging something behind her. No, not dragging exactly. More like assisting the awkwardly shaped sprite by her side. I ran forward into the surf to help her.

"Is that Abhainn?" I asked, shocked at the state of his appearance. His form was shimmering in and out of focus, switching between his human shape and something more akin to the sprites I'd met at Jeremiah's house. His head was misshapen and pointy, his bones protruded from every joint at an unnatural angle, and his legs reminded me of a seabird's.

"*Oui*. He must feed. Now!"

I could hear the queen in her come out. She speaks and expects someone to answer. Ironically we heard a playful scream and round of laughter from further up the shore. Usually it was secluded, but it appeared that a group of teenagers decided to ignore the POSTED signs and risk a trip to the private beach. Human teenagers on the same beach as a hungry sprite. Not a good combination.

"Zhey will do," Isabel said.

"I don't know…" I tried to say but she cut me off.

"He will die! We need a food source now, and zhose ignorant human children are coming zhis way."

She was right. They must have been drunk, because when they saw the three of us standing in the water, one of them shouted and encouraged the others to follow behind. He ran as fast as he could, yelling something about a mermaid. Idiots.

"Fine. But I'm leaving," I said. It wasn't an ideal situation, but in the grand scheme of things I needed Abhainn more right now. A few humans were going to lose their lives for the sake of saving many more tomorrow. "Please come to the house when you are finished. We have much to discuss."

Isabel nodded her head without taking her eyes off of the approaching male. I turned and walked briskly back toward the house. I heard the young man whistle and catcall at Isabel, just before the revolting crunch. A few screams later and everything went silent. Well, the humans did. Abhainn, however, didn't make any attempt to eat politely, and the slurps, snaps, and chomping carried in the wind all of the way to the deck. I shivered in disgust.

Trying to rid my mind of those images, I prepared myself for the meeting. I was pretty sure that we would make a final stand against Lucian tomorrow, but I needed to confirm that the support was there. Adele had many friends, and now that everyone understood what we were fighting against, I hoped they'd be willing to attack.

When I walked into the house, I was met with an eerie silence. Wondering where everyone went, I looked out the front door to see several town cars parked in the driveway, all empty. They must have already arrived.

Knowing there was only one place to go, I hurried down the hall and into the designated conference room. The conversations were in full swing until I walked through the doors.

"Master Matthew, there you are." Adele held out her arms in a surprising show of emotion. We'd worked together for a few months now, but not once had she made an attempt to do any more than shake my hand. I moved to her and offered the embrace she was asking for. Her tiny frame seemed so fragile under my arms, almost like it was on the verge of breaking.

"Thank you for coming, Mistress Lyonetta."

She chuckled. "Please call me Adele. There is little time for formalities these days." She pulled away from me and swept her arm across the conference room. "You will see that we are not alone, Kain. Lucian will not succeed."

I took in my surroundings. Adele brought ten powerful Council members and international clan leaders to the house. Troy had gathered all of the protectors nearby, and Julian called back his selkies. Brendan stood next to Carissa along the side wall, both of them giving me a slight nod when I made eye contact. It probably would have disturbed me more, seeing them side by side, but now was not the time to dwell on such things. I was fairly certain there wouldn't be anything I could do or say to stop Brendan from being a part of this.

"There are several more on the phone," Adele said while walking back to the head of the table. "All of whom are willing to fight back tomorrow."

"This is great," I said. "But do we have a plan?"

Adele smiled at me and the Council members. "We have more than a plan. We have secret weapons." The other leaders nodded in agreement while the rest of us tried to figure out what she was talking about. "Julian has offered the selkies, and we are anticipating you securing the sprites."

"Me?" I asked and then immediately felt like an idiot. "I...I don't know if I can do that."

"Kain, you are the only one who can do this." Carissa stepped forward and my breath caught in my throat. She was so beautiful, and the way she commanded attention was awe inspiring. "My entire clan, along with most of those in France, Italy, Spain, and Japan are making arrangements to send their most powerful leaders to Lucian's tomorrow. The assistance of the selkies is much appreciated, but the merfolk participation was solidified when we promised them the sprites too."

"Well, maybe you shouldn't have done that," I panicked. What if Abhainn and Isabel didn't agree? They were the only sprites I knew. Carissa's faced registered shock for a brief moment before she hid it behind a stoic façade. "I'm sorry," I added quickly. "I just don't know if I can guarantee this."

"Abhainn will do it," Daniel said. I hadn't realized he was in there.

"He will, Kain. All you have to do is ask him." Marisol stepped up next to Daniel and continued to encourage me. "He will do it for you and Eviana."

I looked around the room at all of the expectant faces, waiting for me to agree to this. Instead, I told them the truth. "Abhainn was nearly killed last night." Daniel and Marisol let out a gasp, and several other leaders looked around the table at each other trying to determine if anyone knew about this. "He didn't die," I continued, "but he's not in good shape."

"What about Isabel?" This time it was Brendan who spoke up. I watched him silently ask Julian for the privilege to speak, and when he nodded, Brendan continued. "She is a queen in the ratchet society," he explained to everyone in the room. "You should have seen her in Mexico. She saved a lot of lives by taking control back from Lucian. They listen to her."

I froze. Adele hadn't known about our little rescue mission, although when I glanced at her, she didn't seem like this was new information. If she had learned anything about me in the last few months, she knew where my loyalties stood.

"Who is this Isabel?" someone on the speaker phone asked.

"She is Abhainn's partner," I answered. "She is a ratchet." Most of the leaders took that news in stride. I remembered when Eviana and I met with the clan leaders in this very room not too long ago. We had been surprised that they'd all known about the existence of sprites. It seemed they only left the children out of the loop.

"And they are our friends," Daniel added.

"Is this true?" Adele asked me.

"Yes."

"So will you deliver them to us?"

"I can't deliver anyone, nor would I ever command a sprite to be at our beck and call. They are afraid of our water control abilities. We are the only creature that can harm them." Another look around the room told me that these leaders already knew of the threat we posed to the sprites. I sighed. "I will not command them, but I will ask for their assistance."

"That won't be necessary, lad." Without a sound, Abhainn and Isabel had entered the room and startled us all. Abhainn must have fed well, as he was now in a six foot plus tall, muscular human form that wouldn't have been more than twenty five years old. He'd given himself an expensive dark blue suit and Isabel complimented his style with a skirt and jacket fit for a boardroom. I think it was the first time I saw her fully dressed.

I jumped to my feet and walked over to shake Abhainn's hand. He smiled down at me then took in the room. "Ye will 'ave our assistance. This is as much of an attack on us as it is fer ye. We cannot let him practice The Legacy, and we must act now."

He pulled Isabel closer. "This is Isabella Angeline Fontaine. The queen of the ratchets and our most powerful ally."

Isabel tilted her head in acknowledgement as the others in the room bowed in respect. It was a great feeling to see so many different groups of water creatures getting along. It was exactly what Lucian wanted to avoid.

"And I understand that we have the selkie leader as well?" Adele asked, looking at Julian.

He stepped forward and bowed his head. "Mistress Lyonetta, I am honored to meet you and although we do not have the same social structure amongst our kind, I can assure you that the selkies will fight for me. For us."

"What about those already under Lucian's control?" Troy asked while looking at Malcolm, whether on purpose or not. Troy was still scarred from Malcolm's attack at Lucian's hand.

Julian cringed. "Once they are under the spell, it is difficult for me to call them back. I may need help in those matters."

"Done," Adele said. "Marianne, Andrew, you will assist the selkie leader with your skills. Do what you can to break Lucian's hold and give them back to Julian." The Council leaders agreed.

We spent the next several hours discussing strategy and dividing up duties. By the time everyone left, I felt like we might actually have a chance to beat Lucian. Nearly half of the leaders attending the meeting tomorrow were against Lucian's decree. And now that we had the selkies and the sprites fighting along with us, it would tip the scales in our favor.

Besides, we didn't have another option.

TWENTY

Kain

Since we were going to the Bahamas and Lucian only gave us one day to make plans, each clan decided to charter their own plane, and share seats where necessary. With my real home base just a few hours away in Los Angeles, I managed to procure two larger planes to accommodate me, Marisol, Daniel, and all of the selkie's. Abhainn and Isabel were offered seats, but they said they preferred to travel via water and not thousands of feet in the air.

The plan was relatively simple. Show up and act like we are fulfilling our requested duty, and once everyone was in place, we'd attack. The selkies and sprites would remain in the water, out of Lucian's sight. I didn't doubt that he'd have a patrol guard in the sea, and told Adele as much. She gave Abhainn, Isabel, and Julian the freedom to act as they must to subdue our enemies. Isabel seemed a little too happy about that declaration. Once again, I was thankful she was on our side.

The cross country flight seemed to last forever. Especially when somewhere over Kansas, Brendan decided to move to the seat next to me. I pretended to sleep, but it was futile.

"I can hear your heart beat so I know you're not sleeping," he said without looking at me.

I rotated my head against the seat. "That's really creepy."

He laughed. "I know."

"What do you want?" I tried not to sound annoyed.

"You have to save her, Kain. She needs to get out of this alive." He ran his hands through his hair. It was still hanging in his face, but he used that as a barrier between the two of us. "She deserves to be with you."

That caught me by surprise. It wasn't that I disagreed with him, I just never expected those words to come out of his mouth.

"I am fully prepared to die for her tonight," he continued. I almost told him how melodramic that sounded. "But you have to live. You have to marry her, and love her, and give her a wonderful family…" his voice quivered. "You have to make her forget about me."

I selected my next words very carefully. "She will never forget you, Brendan. But I promise you that I will love her more than anyone else in this world ever could."

He huffed and stared directly at me. "I don't know if that's possible, but thank you for trying." I assumed he was referring to his own feelings for her, but I decided to take the high road and remain quiet.

"Graham Forrester has to die," Brendan said after several moments of uncomfortable silence.

"I agree."

"That should be our job," he continued.

"Okay."

"Okay." It was all he said. We probably should have schemed up some sort of grand plan to take him out, but we didn't. A thousand plans and scenarios were running through my mind and I couldn't come up with one more. We'd just have to wing it.

Brendan moved back to his old seat with the selkies and I endured the rest of the flight suffering in silence. Every minute we got closer, the excitement and fear grew exponentially. The fighter in me, who I recently discovered, was eager for the battle. To conquer one that means to do harm to so many…it would be satisfying to say the least. The Legacy was the old way of doing things in our world centuries ago. Now was the time to move forward.

The clan leader in me feared the deaths that were bound to occur tonight. Lives would be lost, but I had to believe it was still worth it. And lastly, the man in me, the part that loved Eviana and all she stood for, anticipated what our life would be like tomorrow. When this war was finished and we could go back to our homes and our clans, what kind of life would we have? Would she want to get married? Go to college? Our positions somewhat limited our options, but there were always ways around that. Eviana had taught me that much.

I must have fallen asleep thinking about what tomorrow held, because when the plane bounced into the ground, I jumped awake in my seat. Daniel and Marisol, who sat in front of me, turned around and laughed.

"What?" I asked.

"You scream like a little girl," Daniel said. "You must have been having a good dream for that landing to startle you so much."

I glared at him. Had I actually screamed? I kicked the back of his seat, but smiled. I worried about the two of them more than anyone else on this plane. Their skills had yet been tested, but I couldn't force them to stay behind. If I were in their position, I would have wanted to come too.

We walked off the plane and piled into the limousines waiting for us. Julian and the selkies disappeared through the tiny airport hanger presumably to take up their position in the ocean before too many eyes spotted their arrival. We knew that Lucian had spies and assumed we wouldn't be able to keep the selkies a secret forever. But we also had the sprites.

Lucian had cleared out an entire resort on the western side of the island overlooking the calm Caribbean waters. Sunset was only a couple of hours away, and already the pinks and purples were starting to develop on the horizon.

The first thing I noticed when we approached the central area of the resort, was the gazebo decked out in colorful flowers and twinkling lights. This must be for the wedding. Eviana and Graham's wedding.

It wasn't going to happen, but it sent a slice of fear through me anyway. I couldn't stomach the thought of all our planning and coordination failing tonight.

"We will save her." I jumped at the sound of a female voice and the faintest touch on my hand. I turned to see that Adele had sidled up next to me. "Lucian should enjoy his final sunset of this world, for very soon, he will take his last breath."

I'd never heard her speak like that before. It was so cold and calculated. Exactly the way a Council member should be, yet frightening none the same. "What did he do to you?" I asked.

"Do you mean besides stealing Graham out from under my nose?" She shook her head. "I took that boy in when no one else would. I raised him to be *good*. Not the lackey of some disturbed merman. But Graham is an adult and he chose to go down this path. I sincerely hope he won't lose his life for it tonight."

I swallowed hard, remembering the conversation with Brendan on the plane. I seriously doubted that Graham would make it out of this alive.

"But if you're asking what Lucian threatened me with, it was William."

"Who?" I asked.

"My dear, sweet William." I followed her gaze to an older man standing between several selkies on the far side of the gazebo. He wore a dark green cloak, symbolizing his membership on the Northern European Council. As though he felt our focus, he looked up and caught Adele's eyes. They exchanged a look so intimate, I knew that this was her weakness.

She squeezed my hand hard and whispered to me. "He said that he would kill him if I didn't oblige. My first husband died five years ago, and although it was an arranged marriage, we'd grown to love each other. With no children or grandchildren, I thought I'd lost the ability to love when he died. Until I met William. He reinvigorated me. Gave me a reason to enjoy life again." She wiped away the tears in her eyes. "I do believe Graham told him about us. Not many people know." She suddenly stopped speaking. I think it was all too much for her.

"They threatened us, too. Both Lucian and Graham," I added.

"I figured as much," she said then looked up at me and smiled. "I am glad to see that you two finally found your way to each other."

I couldn't help but reciprocate with my own delighted grin. I'd waited so long to have Eviana by my side. There was no alternative, we had to get through the evening.

"There he is," Adele spat and I saw Lucian enter the gazebo like a super star. His long blond hair wafted in the breeze as well as the white silk shirt that hung open at his chest. The man really loved to show off his body. It was gross.

More of his merfolk supporters began to gather around the gazebo. Someone had blocked off a center aisle with that girly stuff used in weddings and bright red flowers. There were no chairs, typical for Lucian to ignore comfort in favor of submission. It seemed to be a thing of his.

"We should prepare," Adele said, then raised up on her toes high enough to kiss my cheek. "I wish you luck."

Before I could thank her, she disappeared amongst the crowd. I found Troy and Palmer in the back of the celebration area. Tonight they wore a business suit in order to blend with the rest of the leaders like myself. We had trained protectors interspersed amongst the Council members as well, hoping that no one would suspect them too soon.

"Did you spot her yet?" I asked Palmer.

"No. But I heard some others saying that the wedding is going to happen first."

"What?" This was not the way we planned the attack. We were going to wait until the meeting was well underway so that Lucian would think everything was going as well as it could. If we waited until after the wedding, then Eviana would officially be married and we may miss our chance completely.

"So you want me to spread the word?" Troy asked, already knowing what was going through my mind.

"Yes, please. We can't let the wedding happen." The surge of excitement turned to apprehension again. This had to work.

"Welcome everyone. Thank you all for coming," Lucian said as though we all had a choice.

"Do it now, please Troy," I whispered and then moved to the aisle. I needed to let Eviana know that we were here.

"Tonight we shall begin with a celebration of a new union and a new way of life." His supporters clapped and yelled and glared at those who weren't. "I am honored to wed my daughter to one of the most promising young men our kind has ever had the privilege of knowing."

Lucian lifted his arm to the side and Graham climbed up onto the gazebo to join him. He smiled at his almost father-in-law. "Graham and Eviana will lead us into a great new revolution. Their abilities far surpass the rest of us, and their children will only be that much stronger."

My stomach dropped. *Children?*

"So without further ado, let's make this union official." Music began to play from somewhere and I picked up the pace to reach the center aisle. We were packed on the patio like sardines in a can, and even though I tried to be polite at first, by the time the band reached the chorus of the classical wedding song, I was throwing elbows left and right to get through.

I'd almost reached the last row when I saw her. Gliding down the patio stairs was the vision I'd replayed in my head over and over for years. Eviana in a white wedding dress, walking toward me. Although in this case, her face was wrinkled in consternation and her eyes were puffy from crying. I still found her beautiful and it was that beauty which prevented me from saving her.

"You!" Someone yelled behind me just before I felt a hand slam into my mouth and an arm wrap around chest. I tried to fight it, but soon three more sets of hands held me still. "Say one word and she dies," the voice whispered into my ear.

Wasn't anyone witnessing this? Didn't they see me being attacked? I tried to turn my head but it was held too tight. The guards dragged me backward through the crowd who now cleared a pathway for me. I caught a glimpse of Palmer out of the corner of my eye, and tried to convey that he stay hidden. We still had numbers on our side. It wasn't worth giving that up just yet.

I stopped struggling with the protectors. Lucian was smart. He knew I couldn't control our own kind or the selkies very well. It was a win win for him.

Someone punched me in the stomach, surprising me and pissing me off in the same instant. But I didn't fight back. It wasn't time yet. I fell to my knees, effectively offering my surrender. After one more kick to the ribs, all except for one of the protectors left, leaving me alone on the ground listening to Eviana's wedding progress.

Twenty One

Eviana

Where was Kain? I looked over the crowd a hundred times trying to find my strength. I needed him to be here. I needed to know there was a plan to stop this nonsense. And I was running out of time.

After my visit with the nereid, Lucian and Graham brought me back to the house where I'd slept through the night and late into the next day. My dreams were vivid and colorful that evening, and I wasn't sure what was real or make believe when I woke up in the morning.

Lucian didn't waste any time. He forced me to practice on the protectors first to see if I could compel the mermen. It was almost as easy as the selkies. I barely had to force the command, and could instead whisper it in my head to have them succumb. In one visit with the nereid, my life had changed dramatically. I became my father.

Graham worked with me and the water control. On several instances he laughed when my tendrils attempted to squeeze his throat.

He thought I was playing around, while I was really fine tuning my aim. I had no desire to be married to Graham. And if the wedding did happen, I wouldn't stay married very long.

By four in the afternoon on the second day, Lucian demanded I stop practicing and get ready for the ceremony. I refused to call it my wedding. He'd ushered me into a private villa at the resort complex, where three human women were waiting to serve my every request. It was obvious that Lucian had brainwashed them into thinking this was a joyous occasion, and when they finally left, I watched him perform another round of compulsion.

It was too much pressure for me to keep pretending this was a perfect day, so I had asked the ladies to leave before putting on my dress. Still, Lucian had done it again. The gown was perfect for someone who wanted to get married, and just what a doting father would buy his daughter for her special day. A simple spaghetti strap top with a fitted bodice flowed into layers upon layers of chiffon. Tiny crystals were sewn into the dress all over, so that when the light hit it just the right way, I sparkled like the stars. The women had curled my hair into ringlets and let it fall naturally all around. It hung past my waist now, which meant it could almost cover the single black orchid I was being forced to carry.

"You will go through with it all, Eviana, or I will kill your merman piece by piece," Lucian threatened me just after swooning over how beautiful I looked. He was beyond crazy.

Since Graham wasn't allowed to see me, and Lucian needed to "greet the vassals", I would walk down the aisle by myself. Thinking this may be an opportunity to act, I agreed. But when I reached the main lobby area for which I needed to pass through to the courtyard, I saw that Lucian made sure a security detail watched my every move. I probably would have been able to control one or two, but I didn't think I could hold all of them at once. Plus I had to assume Kain and the others would have a plan.

So when I started that dreaded march to my social demise, I frantically wanted to see his face. One look to assure me that we were going to get away from here. For a moment I thought I saw him, but the crowd quickly pushed together to get a closer view of the ceremony and I accepted that my mind was playing tricks on me.

A string quartet played a classical piece I recognized but didn't know the name of. The music should have calmed me, but it had the complete opposite effect. My palms leaked with sweat all over the stupid flower I had to carry. If my heart beat any faster, I believed that it would go into cardiac arrest. Maybe that could be my way out.

I saw Lucian standing next to Graham at the end of the aisle and in the center of the gazebo, glaring at me. I was taking too long. I couldn't help it if my feet wouldn't move, could I? Lucian made a small sign with his hand that was only for my eyes. The fake knife across the throat, disguised by a touch to his hair, let me know that he was insinuating death again.

I was really tired of being threatened.

A few moments later I reached the gazebo steps. To my right sat Lucian's drones. His supporters that would stop at nothing to betray their kind. And to my left was everyone else. I saw Adele Lyonetta and we shared a moment. Her face looked tired and worn, but her eyes were anything but. There was a plan, I knew it.

Lucian cleared his throat, forcing me to look up at him and my husband to be. Had the situation been in a parallel world without kidnappings, betrayal, and my biological father, I may have been happy to marry Graham. His handsome face captivated me for the briefest of moments until I remembered that it was just the blood talking. Still, he looked amazing in his black suit which hugged his frame in all the right places.

He smiled at me like he knew where my thoughts had drifted. Deciding that I was tired of playing along, I glared back. Lucian immediately walked forward and yanked me up to the makeshift altar. He squeezed my arm hard, for sure leaving a mark.

"Behave," he whispered in my ear without even moving his lips. In fact, he smiled the entire time.

"You could at least pretend to love me," Graham said in a mocking tone. "I love you."

"You have no idea what love is," I spat back. Lucian quickly began his speech to cover the noise of our argument.

"Ladies and gentlemen. Leaders of our kind. It gives me great honor to present my daughter, Eviana Anne Duhmal to be wed to Graham Marcus Forrester on this night, in the presence of all." Lucian lifted my hand and firmly placed it into Graham's. He smiled and I fought back tears.

"The union of these two commanding individuals will secure the future of our kind." I tried to pull my hand away from Graham, but he held fast and sent a cunning wink in my direction. I dug my nails into his skin.

"If anyone here should wish to deny these two their birthrights and destined union, now would be the time to speak."

I frantically looked around the crowd, particularly those on my side of the gathering, but no one said a word. Where was Kain? Or Troy? *Someone.* Someone had to stop this.

"Very well, and excellent choice..." Lucian's voice cracked. "Excellent..." he tried to finish, but began coughing instead. Clearing his throat, he started again. "As I was saying, agreeing to this union is a wise..."

This time, he grabbed at his chest and began sucking in shallow, raspy breaths. The crowd started to whisper and move about, wondering what was happening. Lucian's protectors ran to the gazebo and caught him under the arms.

"Master Sutherland, what's wrong?"

Lucian continued to gasp, but his eyes were scanning the crowd. When they reached their target, I saw his face contort into rage. "Her!"

We all looked in the direction his hand was pointing and I nearly cried with joy. Adele had removed herself from the masses and was now standing in the front, staring at Lucian. It took a moment for me to realize that she was controlling something within him.

"You are not the only one with power, Lucian. Now!"

Her command brought a flurry of action. Almost at once, the left side of the audience attacked the right. Our supporters finally enacted their revenge on Lucian's cronies.

Fists flew, compulsion wars began, and I stood there. Frozen. It probably wasn't for very long, but time seemed to stand still. As if in slow motion, I watched our side fight with an amazing show of strength and force that Lucian's new friends didn't stand a chance. However, the weaker ones in the horde were easily taken down by mental commands. I only caught a glimpse, but I looked on in horror as Marisol dropped to her knees in front of Elizabetta, one of Lucian's new Council members. She was forcing them to obey left and right until an entire cluster of merfolk surrounded her. As one, they moved through the crowd, her protective circle blocking an intruder then turning them into a puppet like the others.

Daniel screamed. I'm not sure how I knew it was Daniel, but I did. His voiced sliced through the night, even though I couldn't spot him. Tears streamed down my cheeks and I yelled out in frustration. I looked for Kain, yet couldn't find him. My heart hammered in my chest until I finally saw two other familiar faces.

Troy and Palmer fought with the new Council's assigned protectors, leaving a wide gap between them and Elizabetta who continued to squash those around her like bugs. They were doing a great job at defending themselves and working together as a team to accomplish their goals. In the few seconds I managed to see, they had subdued five protectors.

Lucian dropped to the ground and hacked until I thought an organ would fall out. Adele moved closer, never breaking her concentration. She was actually winning.

That was until an older merman in a dark green cloak appeared by her side. Lucian smiled and stopped coughing long enough to turn his head and look up at Graham. They exchanged a look so evil that I knew what came next would not bode well for Adele.

"No!" I shouted, but it was too late. Graham had already seized control of the old man, who was now beating his own head and face. I saw the glistening tears in Adele's eyes, but she tried not to look away from Lucian. He coughed again, this time spitting up blood.

The old man fell to the ground, hard enough to break bones. His head slammed against the concrete patio, then he went still. Adele yelled out and dropped to help him, severing her hold on Lucian.

"Get her out of here," he growled at Graham.

"No! Help!" I yelled, hoping someone would hear me. With all of the commotion and fighting and compulsion going on, I knew it would be useless.

"Eviana!" It seemed like a trick; not a real voice. "Eviana!"

Kain had found me.

"Kain!" I yelled back, not sure where he was coming from. Graham dragged me by my hair backward over the far side of the gazebo and down to the beach. "Kain!"

We stumbled past battles between mermaids, mermen, protectors, and leaders. Our supporters appeared to be corralling the others toward the water's edge. Why would they do that? They might be able to hold their own on land, but it would be tough to compete with an element controlling leader in the water.

I fell to the ground and screamed when Graham pulled on my hair. "Shut up!" he snapped. "Get up, now!"

"Kain!" I didn't hear him anymore. The multitude of fights drowned out any chance of me finding his beautiful voice. I started to cry.

And then I felt the warm, inviting water wash over my legs. I don't know why I hadn't realize this sooner, but being in the water might just give me the edge I needed to get away from Graham.

"Mistress Dumahl!"

Someone called for me but it wasn't Kain this time. Turning my face toward the sea, I felt my heart swell. A giant sprite head bobbed along the surface, showing me the mouthful of dangerous incisors. I couldn't remember the last time I had been so happy to see Abhainn. He survived and if he was here, that meant the ratchets were too.

As Graham dragged me backward into the water, I watched in silence while Lucian's followers were forced into the ocean. They changed into mermaid form quickly, but many of them never surfaced again. I knew the water sprites were having a feast tonight.

Several streams of water exploded around us, as the losing team began to fight for their last breath. Tendrils controlled by the merfolk snaked across the surface, latching on to ratchet necks and squeezing them until they burst. That only sent the sprites into a frenzy and soon, merfolk body parts flew through the air.

I swallowed the bile in my throat and decided that I was tired of Graham controlling my every move. Reaching up behind me, I focused on him harder than I'd ever concentrated on anything before. *Release me!* I commanded in my head. For a brief moment, his grip loosened. I pulled my hair free and stood in the knee deep water to face him. In the quickest way possible, I drew the water up from the surface and attempted to wrap it around his throat, just as I'd been practicing the last two days.

For a second, he froze in terror. But when I saw the smirk snake its way through his features, fear slammed me in the gut. I wasn't strong enough yet.

He jumped at me and managed to push us both into the surf. The water pounded against our bodies, nearly drowning me in the process. The only thing I could do was change.

The dress would have normally been an obstacle, but tonight my legs shifted freely without the need to shred my clothing. In seconds, I felt the final tingle and lifted my tail hard into Graham who was still pinning me down.

The impact knocked him over my head, so I dove into the water and began to swim. Somewhere in my peripheral, I could sense others following. But at this moment, I needed to put some distance between Graham and me.

After several minutes, or maybe it was seconds, of swimming, I stopped to see where he was. Some instinct was encouraging me to do so. My wedding gown weighed me down, yet the adrenaline kept me afloat. I looked around the surface, trying to take in the situation. Just past the surf, and moving fast in my direction, I noticed the wall of water.

The tactic was undeniably Graham's, but it was Kain I saw first. There, on the beach, was my Kain. He held out both hands like he was commanding somebody to stop, but his focus was entirely on the wall moving toward me.

I only had a moment to wonder why he was sending the water in my direction, when I saw him. Graham exploded from the surface five feet in front of me, in full merman form, and slammed against my chest. I could barely grasp a breath before we plummeted into the dark waters.

Graham's hands tightened around my arms as we hurdled down and away from the scene on the beach. My shoulder slammed into a piece of coral, slicing it open and forcing the burning salt water inside. I tried to scream, but then realized I didn't have much air in my lungs. If we didn't surface soon, I worried for my survival.

Feeling the cool, yet painful sting of my blood leaving my body, I attempted to knock my head into Graham's chest. But with the way he was holding me, almost like a surf board, I couldn't reach an area on him that would do any type of harm.

The sudden, piecing howl sent a wave of relief through me. There was simply no mistaking the war cry of a selkie.

In a whirl of motion, Graham was knocked away and something nudged me in the side. The seal head banged against me several times before I had enough sense to swim up to the surface. I knew without looking that Brendan was here.

I wouldn't be able to describe the range of emotions my heart experienced at that moment. After all we'd been through, after his instinctual nature prevailed, Brendan was still trying to save me.

When I didn't move fast enough, he nudged me in the direction he wanted to go. First, I needed to get to the surface, so instead of going to the side as he requested, I headed straight up to catch a breath of salty air. The mumbled sounds beneath the sea suddenly exploded into an orchestra of battle noises. Yelling, fighting, the cracking of burning buildings all caught my attention at the shoreline. Where did the fire come from?

It was the briefest of thoughts, but for some reason I was fixated on it. Perhaps that was because it reminded me of the night Graham and I escaped Lucian's attack at Jeremiah's. Part of his house had burned along with the sleeping quarters of so many human servants. It had been my first encounter with ratchets and it had changed my opinion of the world I lived in.

Brendan suddenly bit down hard on my arm and pulled me further away from the shore. His teeth hurt, yet I was temporarily lost in the past and incapable of moving forward. Within a few minutes, my back hit shallow ground. It woke me up out of my haze and I looked around wondering why I was on land this far out in the ocean.

Brendan released his hold on my arm, but continued to nudge my side. Rolling over so that I could see in front of me, I pulled myself up onto the narrow sandbar. Why did he push me here? This was land, not sea. As if reading my thoughts, Brendan barked at me. It was a sound unique to him and I knew what it meant. *Change.*

I closed my eyes and willed my legs back to me. It took way too long, and I began to panic. A warm, furry body sidled up to me, instantly putting my mind at ease. Brendan had always been able to comfort me with one touch, and now I felt like I needed him more than ever.

He nestled against me and growled. It wasn't a mean growl, it was more like a purr. *Relax Eviana*, it meant. And so I relaxed.

The prickly sand grains pressing through my toes was the first feeling I noticed when my legs returned. Although shaky, I used them to sit back on my knees. Brendan looked at me for a moment, then placed his seal head in my lap. I couldn't help but stroke his fur while all of our years together danced through my mind. The first time we met, our first kiss, the night in the mountain lodge…all of the wonderful memories we'd shared.

He had been a part of my life for so long, and now he was back in it. Saving me. Protecting me. A new hole opened in my heart and I began to sob uncontrollably. Resting my head against his, I held Brendan in my arms, with no intention of letting him leave. He whimpered and tried to pull away, but I wouldn't let him. I couldn't let him go so easily.

"Well, isn't that a sight." Graham said as he emerged from the water and walked along the sand bar. His pants were missing, but the white wedding shirt remained. He shook the water off his head, and smirked. "Too bad this will be your last moment together."

I didn't have time to register the threat before a wave swallowed us both.

TWENTY TWO

Eviana

I tumbled over backward, the ground skimming my legs and the water swallowing me whole. Reaching out for Brendan, I barely caught a glimpse of his form and a touch of his hair, before being ripped away from him again. It took several moments of being tossed around like a stone before I could orient myself, and by then, my body was battered and nearly broken.

The rumbling of the churning water drowned out all other sounds. In its own way, it was peaceful. I was meant to be under the water, it was in my nature. But the constant feeling of defeat was not something I would ever be accustomed to.

Just as I decided to take back control of my fate, the water suddenly disappeared. I stopped rolling against the ground and sucked in a deep, energizing breath. Landing on my back, I opened my eyes to see that the water hadn't vanished, it was instead hovering in the air around me. Had I done that?

Someone grunted nearby, but the water surrounding me blocked the view. I heard a shout, followed by the unmistakable sound of a fist hitting skin. Without much thought, I stood and forced the water to fall to the sides. Finally free of the element, I could see how isolated we really were on this sand bar. The shoreline was still visible, but when I was knocked backward in that wave, I'd been pushed further out to sea.

Standing ankle deep in water, I struggled to find the source of the commotion nearby. Two men fighting in the distance made an eerie silhouette against the flames burning brightly on the beach. They were too far away for me to notice who was winning, but in my gut I knew Kain and Graham wouldn't stop until one of them was dead.

That thought dropped me to my knees as the pit in my stomach ripped open. Kain couldn't die. Not for me. Not ever.

I had to end this.

Swallowing the fear, and pain, and worry pulsing throughout my body, I forced myself to stand and began to move toward them. A small wave, one not caused by a merman, rushed up against my legs causing me to stumble. Something large and furry landed in front of my shins, making me jump over it. However, I wasn't quick enough, and I ended up stepping on top of him instead.

"Brendan?" Still in his seal form, he seemed to wake up and take in the situation. I kneeled down next to him to look for injuries. There weren't any obvious bites or tears, but he was disoriented and slow in his movements. "Are you okay?"

I'll never forget the look in those green eyes for the rest of my life. He stared at me with such intensity, such love, that it settled deep into my soul. Never to be thrown out or forgotten again.

I sat down, unable to breath and unable to stand. Brendan crawled a little closer so that his flippers straddled both of my legs. Although initially serious, his eyes now twinkled with mischief. Again I was reminded of the very first time we met. The world disappeared around us for the briefest of moments while stared at each other's eyes.

Kain's scream ended everything. I remembered that there was someone else in my life now. I remembered that Brendan left me and we would never be together again. And I remembered that we had to help Kain.

Brendan must have noticed the change in my expression, because he narrowed his eyes at me and snarled. He wanted me to stay out of it.

"No way. I need to help him!" Wiggling backward, I tried to get out from under the two hundred pound seal. He barked in my face. "Get off of me, Brendan!"

Kain yelled again, only this time the end was cut off with gurgling sounds. Brendan turned toward them and then back to me. He huffed and hung his head. It confused me for a minute, until his eyes caught mine again. I swear they shimmered with fresh tears, even though I didn't know selkies could cry in their animal form.

Brendan leaned forward and touched the tip of his snout against my nose. He brushed it lightly from side to side, giving me his seal version of a kiss. It felt like a lifetime since I'd last had that kind of touch from him. Without thinking, I lifted my arm to pet the top of his head, and closed my eyes for one quick second. I knew right then that a part of me would always love him.

When I opened my eyes, Brendan was gone. I glimpsed his back flippers disappearing off the edge of the sand bar and into the sea. He was heading straight for the two mermen and I panicked. Brendan wouldn't stand a chance against Graham's compulsion.

Demanding my legs to work, I ran toward the three guys in my life. For good or bad, they were all connected to me and all fighting for me in different ways. It was time that I stood up for myself.

I'd almost reached the far side of the sandbar, when I realized why Kain had been yelling. He had managed to trap Graham's legs in a cyclone of water, but he was holding his head and howling in pain. Just as I got close enough to attack, the last of Kain's water drizzled back into the surf. Graham's focus intensified and Kain began to sink into the sand.

"Enough!" I yelled at Graham. He flew backward through the air so quickly I didn't even know what happened. When his body slammed into the ground, he actually laughed.

"Nice work, tart." It wasn't more than a whisper, but using his nickname for me sent me into a rage. I ran forward and jumped on his stomach. It surprised him enough that I was able to get two quick punches to his face before he caught my hands. "We'll have time to role play later. But for now I must ask you to stop ruining the best part of my body."

I couldn't believe he wasn't taking this seriously. I began to push the back of his head into the ground, trying to will the water to swallow him whole. As soon as he realized what I was doing, a look crossed his face that sent fear running through me.

He wrapped both of his hands around my throat and squeezed. It wasn't time to use compulsion or water control, he was simply trying to kill me. "I thought we would be happy together, Eviana. You know how much I've wanted you since the day we met in Seattle. Why couldn't you make the right choice?"

He squeezed harder. I tried to pull his hands away at the same time I reached deep into my mind for the ability to control others. But my brain was fighting for oxygen right now and it wouldn't focus on the task at hand.

"Really, tart. I feel like killing you is such a waste." In my weakened state, he was able to roll me off of him so that he now straddled my waist. It gave him much better traction for the strangulation posture. He pushed down. "I asked, no *begged* Lucian to keep you alive, but he insisted that you would be a problem if you didn't submit."

I clawed at his face, tried to kick his legs, but nothing worked. My body was shutting down. I managed to catch a glimpse of Kain, buried chest deep in the sand and completely unconscious. How had Graham done that?

Stars. I saw stars above my face. Some were real in the sky, others flitted by as the last of my will to fight disintegrated into a haze. For a second, I thought that this end was fitting. Lucian would not have me. Graham would not have me. In my own way, I was going to win.

A large shadow flew over top of me and slammed into Graham, knocking his hands away and pulling me back into this world. It hurt like hell. My lungs burned and screamed for oxygen, yet when I opened my mouth to inhale that much needed air, every muscle in my throat seized in pain. I wondered if Graham had broken something; my windpipe, my spine, my will to survive. No, I couldn't let this happen.

In the amount of time it took for me to recover, Brendan and Graham had created a bloodbath. Literally. The water splashing around our legs had a darkened tint to it that only blood can produce. I could even smell the metallic flavor in the sea spray.

When my eyes finally focused, I watched Graham slam his hand into Brendan's side. He yelped in pain as Graham repeated the same motion over and over. At one point, the light from the beach fire glimmered off the knife the he was plunging relentlessly into my selkie. Where did he get a knife?

I crawled toward them, still unable to speak or breathe very well, but someone grabbed my ankle. Kain, buried in the sand, shook his head and stopped me from helping Brendan. Before I could ask if he was crazy, he squeezed his eyes shut and started to lift from the ground. Even in the dark I could see the moisture of the dampened sand disappear while Kain forced it to move his body out of the trap.

Brendan snarled and this time Graham screamed out in pain. The two of them twisted and turned in a horrifying dance that wouldn't end well. I tried to step closer again, but Kain wrapped his arms around my chest and held me back. I felt the empty knife sheath on his waist and panicked.

"Let go," I shouted, but it only came out as a hoarse whisper.

"No, we cannot help them."

I swung my head around to look up into his face. "What are you talking about?" Just then, I heard it. The sound that water makes right before a wave peaks. The deep rumbling of power.

Brendan's teeth sank into Graham's neck moments before the two of them were encircled by angry water. The globe trapped them both and sent them hurdling away from us and down the sand bar.

I think what happened next only lasted a few seconds, but it would forever change my life.

Brendan ripped out Graham's throat. The merman grabbed for the hole, but was unable to slow his death. It came quickly and horribly. I could barely see it through the water, but just as Brendan seemed to have won, he dropped to the ground and sucked in a large amount of liquid.

The aqueous barrier disappeared, and Kain couldn't stop me from running toward them. I reached Graham first, and although we'd shared a few intimate moments in our brief life together, I jumped over his corpse and dove to the ground next to Brendan.

His seal skin now rested over a human body as though he were taking a nap. Blood seeped out from several wounds, with the worst one being just above his heart.

"Brendan," I cried and threw off his skin. What I saw stopped me cold. Graham's knife had pierced through every opening between his ribs. Part of his internal organs were showing, and the blood pumping from his heart began to slow. "No, no, no."

Kain fell to the ground next to me and placed his hands over Brendan's heart, trying to stop the bleeding. I sat there and cried. We were not going to be able to save him, and only a few seconds later, Brendan left me forever.

My world stopped being. My heart seemed to stop beating and I stopped living. Brendan was dead. He died fighting for me and after all of the bad things that happened between us, I didn't think I could survive his death. It was one thing to know that he left me yet was still in this world, it was another to lose him completely.

My gut ached with longing. Brendan had been a part of me for so much of my life, I simply couldn't imagine him not existing anymore.

"Eviana?" Kain's heavy arm wrapped over my shoulders, but I really didn't feel anything. The weight of the world already pulled me down. "Eviana, we have to go."

I snapped my head in Kain's direction, annoyed that he wanted to leave so quickly after Brendan had just died. When he saw my look he tensed up, but then pointed in the other direction. Abhainn was floating above the surface, just past where the sand bar dropped off, waiting for us.

"I am very sorry, Mistress Dumahl," he said. "But we must get ye to shore. Now."

I couldn't speak, but somehow I moved. I don't remember exactly how I did it, but I reached down and gave Brendan's beautiful face one last kiss, then grabbed his skin. Kain gave me a look that I ignored. I wasn't ready to let go completely just yet, and they could keep their opinions to themselves for all that I cared.

I walked into the sea deep enough to change and dove head first under the surface hugging all that I had left of Brendan tightly against my chest.

Twenty Three

Eviana

The silence under the water should have calmed my senses, but instead it infuriated me. Was everyone dead? All of the ratchets that fought for our cause? All of Lucian's supporters? Was this war finally over?

I had my answer the moment we reached the shore. Bodies littered the beach, some moving and groaning, other still. The once romantic resort had been reduced to a battlefield reminiscent of years past. Several of the private villas looked like they'd weathered a hurricane, while the gazebo continued to burn. Even though the scene was disturbing in so many ways, my focus couldn't be deterred.

I walked from the ocean, transitioning as soon as my tail brushed the bottom. Dragging behind me like a symbol of my fury, Brendan's seal skin splashed in the waves. I don't know why I carried it really, I guess I couldn't let it go. I felt Kain and Abhainn hovering behind me, but I only had eyes for one merman.

Those left standing in the crowd had formed a semicircle around Lucian, who waited patiently for my arrival. His back was toward the flames, yet I could still see that his hair hung wildly around his shoulders, and his chest was covered in scrapes and cuts. He leaned on a long sword shining against the background.

I marched up closer to him, ignoring Kain and Abhainn's warning to stay back. As I got within ten feet of my biological and psychotic father, I noticed the rest of the preparations he'd made.

On their knees in front of the brooding merman, were what was left of my friends and family. Marisol's black eye and swollen lips made her almost unrecognizable. She sobbed and shuttered like it was her last day on this planet. Daniel's face was hard and determined despite the fact that he cradled his arm I was sure would be broken. Troy and Palmer slumped against the ground, unconscious and possibly dead. To the side, Julian stood with Malcolm, but their focus was on Lucian. He had them under his control.

"I brought you a present, daughter." He waved his arms around in front of him. "I must say that I am quite impressed with the efforts here tonight, but you all need learn your place now." He looked around the crowd. "And I think I will start with her."

A protector pushed his way forward, towing a woman behind with little care for her well being. He tossed Adele Lyonetta to the ground in front of Lucian. I knew I should have felt something, but my emotions were so numbed by Brendan's death that I failed to harness the energy.

"This woman is no longer your leader. She has committed treason by directly attacking me this evening and for that she will pay." He raised his sword and prepared to swing. Adele's eyes met mine just before she smiled. If I hadn't been looking for it, I never would have noticed her slight nod. At first I thought she was accepting her impending death, but then I saw her mouth something to Kain.

He grabbed my hand and squeezed so hard, I snapped back into action. Lucian's sword swung in slow motion while I commanded him to stop. Even when practicing the last couple of days, I'd only been able to get partial control over Lucian. He was too strong.

But this time, I had Kain. His strength flowed through me like a warm blanket and an electrical pulse of power. In one hand, I held on to a symbol of my past that fueled the hatred I had toward Lucian. And in the other, I held my future.

With the assistance of Kain's energy, I felt like I could compel the world. Everything around me disappeared aside from Lucian and his swinging sword. I threw out all of my focus on his actions and commanded him to stop. It was like I could almost see the compulsion explode from my body, cross the sandy beach, and dissolve into Lucian's head. The time for sticky hands and glowing minds was over. My power now resembled a lightning strike; deadly accurate and powerfully destructive.

In slow motion, Lucian lifted his eyes to meet my fierce gaze. I could see the disbelief cross his features at the same time he dropped the sword, inches away from Adele's neck. No one interfered, and no one spoke. Or if they did, their words were dead to me. I screamed in frustration when I felt Brendan's seal skin brush against my leg. With that, came another push of my compulsion, and almost every merfolk, selkie, and sprite on the beach dropped to their knees.

I vaguely remember looking over at Kain and wondering why he was still standing, but the errant thought floated away when I refocused on Lucian.

"You do not win!" I yelled at him. "You will no longer torment us, threaten us, or rule over us! You are finished!"

My throat hurt, my heart hurt, but the anger inside of me dulled all of the pain. I was seeing red. Images of my parents, my uncle, the Shannons, Jeremiah, and Brendan swarmed my vision, almost causing me to lose my balance. Too many had died at the hands of this man.

Lucian Sutherland, the manipulating mastermind who single-handedly destroyed my family and so many others, knelt before me like an obedient dog. In a haze, I moved toward him, feet sinking into the sand, my wedding gown dripping with seawater and whipping in the wind. With Brendan's skin wrapped tightly in my left hand, I broke contact with Kain. The power surging through me didn't cease. So I embraced it.

Lucian's sword lay just out of reach of fallen merman, but he never made a move. I had total control over his mind and body and for the first time, I relished in that feeling. Bending forward, I picked up the sword. It was heavier than I imagined. The steel blade reflected the reds and oranges of the fire behind us, and the dark pits of shadows encircling us all. I lifted the sword up high and stared at it. Could I do it? Could I kill him?

"Eviana?" Kain asked. He hadn't moved, but he was still immune to my compulsion. I cocked my head to the side trying to put together a cohesive thought. Brendan's skin tingled in my hand so I held it up next to my chest. I think I shed tears, but I still couldn't feel everything. There was pain in there, deep inside the pit of my stomach, and I couldn't let it out just yet.

The only semblance of emotion I could fathom was revenge. Lucian had to die tonight.

I placed the sword in his hand and commanded him to rise. He complied and awaited his next order. Lucian had to die tonight, but I didn't have to be the one to do it. With a quick force of words in his head, I set us all free from his torturous reign. He plunged the sword into his chest, piercing his heart, and ending his life for good.

"Eviana!" Kain shouted and ran toward me.

"Gather the rest of them and do what you will to end this," I said to Adele and anyone else who would listen. My head throbbed and my legs gave out. I was so tired.

The moment I broke my hold on my audience, Elizabetta screamed and attacked the closet mermaid to her which was a costly mistake. Adele took one look at Elizabetta and forced the water in her cells, tissues, and organs, to suffocate her faster than I would have thought possible. The beautiful creature fell to the ground, face twisted into a panicked look that would stay there forever. No one else attacked after that.

I felt a pair of warm, strong arms wrap around me and hold tight. "Eviana, I'm here," Kain whispered in my ear. "I'm here."

Realizing it was over, I began to sob. Brendan's skin fell limply over my lap, causing me to cry louder and faster. Another set of arms joined us, followed by several more. Marisol nestled up against me and

Daniel hugged my back. I think Palmer and Abhainn even joined in. The feeling of comfort and peace overwhelmed me. After everything that happened, we were going to make it out okay. Or at least some of us were.

The last thing I remembered was the body of Lucian, on his knees and tilted forward, resting on the hilt of his sword. We'd ended this war, and I could finally rest.

I closed my eyes and let the blackness surround me.

Three days later, we gathered on the beach in front of my house to say goodbye to Brendan. Malcolm and Julian had been seriously injured in the fight, but with Julian's master selkie status, they managed to make their way here. Troy was one of the few protectors to survive. He'd saved Palmer from that fate as well, and I would forever be grateful.

I'd remained unconscious until late in the night, and after Adele managed to take control of the situation. Most of the merfolk still siding with Lucian decided to step down and accepted Adele's offer to rejoin their communities in return for complete support. The other choice had been death. Still, half of the merfolk leaders who had attended Lucian's little celebration lost their lives. Isabel reported that a dozen ratchets were killed, and one selkie died. My celtic.

I'd functioned in a haze since we left the islands and returned home. Life continued on. Even this new life post Lucian and the brutal merfolk war that needed to hidden from humans. The bodies on the beach were removed and dumped at sea. The resort received a hefty donation for repairs for the unfortunate "lightning strike" and subsequent storm damage. With the loss of so many merfolk leaders, a new regime was evolving. I knew I would have to play my part in it all, but today was reserved for Brendan.

"Does anybody have anything else they'd like to say?" Daniel asked. His eyes were puffy and his nose red. He'd loved Brendan too, even after all that had happened.

We stood in a small circle an hour before sunset, looking down at a picture of Brendan. It had been taken on this very beach a year ago. His green eyes shown in the sunlight and his smile brightened the entire day. It was one of the only photos I had. His body stayed behind in the Bahamas, taken far enough out into the deep waters that it would never be seen again. Julian promised me that it was the way of the selkies and I had to accept that he would have wanted to finish his life underwater.

I still held his skin in my arms, refusing to let it go just yet. "Thank you all for this," I whispered. Kain smiled at me across the circle, and Marisol squeezed my hand. "I'm going to go now."

After a round of hugs and silent goodbyes to Brendan's picture, I turned and walked to the surf. The late afternoon sun warmed my face as the gulls overhead called to me.

"Are you sure you don't want me to come with you?" Kain's quiet approach startled me.

"No, I'm okay." I leaned into his chest. "I need to do this alone." He kissed the top of my head and lingered there for several long moments. I knew that he was worried about me, but I would heal eventually. Today would be the first step.

Kain left my side but I waited until he disappeared behind the dunes before moving again. For a brief second, I dropped Brendan's skin, giving me just enough time to step out of my dress. Scooping up the only piece of him I had left into my arms, I walked underneath the surf.

Many days and nights, I would swim these waters to meet Brendan at our sanctuary. The rocky island became ours shortly after he moved to California to be near me. Now, I was returning there to say my final goodbyes.

I almost thought that the ocean knew I was grieving today. The kelp seemed to stand still, the otters swam leisurely around my flanks. No one wanted to play. As I approached the rocky shore, my heart climbed into my throat. An overwhelming wave of grief tugged at my stomach, threatening to pull it free.

I swallowed the lump and fought back the tears, as I demanded my legs to form and support the weight of the day. With his skin in hand, I walked to the far edge of the rock formation, where the sheer face plummeted straight down. The sun always reflected a thousand colors off of the shards, but today seemed to be only shades of red.

Choosing a final resting spot for his skin, I laid it down next to the wall and on top of a large boulder. Not knowing what to say, I stood still until the sun was just about to set. Too much had passed between us to sum up in words. I'd loved Brendan for so long and so deeply that I guessed there would always be a hole in my heart.

Only time would heal the gaping wounds left in our world. Loved ones were lost, a new leadership was developing. Policies, Council members, our relationship with humans…it was all about to change. Each day would bring a new beginning and each day we would get a little bit closer to being whole.

I kissed my hand and gently rested it against Brendan's skin. *Goodbye*, I thought, and turned to walk back to the water. Breathing in deep, I closed my eyes and prepared to move on. It wasn't going to be easy, but I knew that I had friends and family who would be there for me, and we would survive this together.

As the final glimmer of orange retreated beneath the horizon, I vanished under the sea to begin my new life.

EPILOGUE

One Year Later

"Hurry up!" Marisol squeaked. I watched her stumble over a shoe and curse when she stubbed her toe against the ground.

"I told you that dress was too long," Daniel teased, and then quickly dodged a flying object. I think it was my hairbrush.

"You two aren't helping me." I couldn't get the back of my dressed hooked, and they were too busy picking fights with each other to realize this. "I guess we'll just have to cancel."

"No!" they both shouted together. I laughed.

"You are not getting out of this one, Eviana." Daniel immediately began working on the final few clasps and I tried not to breathe so they would pull together. "You are going to have this wedding today, no matter what. I don't care if there is a nuclear attack, this is happening."

"Besides, you're all dressed up now, it would be a shame to waste the day," Marisol said while she fastened my necklace and fluffed my hair.

I had a feeling she was more concerned with people not seeing her new gown, but then again she had grown up quite a bit in the past year. She was completely obsessed with Quinlan, and I knew she was counting the days until she could have her wedding. But she had also stepped up into a leadership role with me. I'd put her in charge of organizing the youth programs for our clan, and she was doing a wonderful job. My parents would have been so proud of her. I was proud of her.

"Thank you," I said and quickly kissed her cheek. She pulled back in mock disgust, but I saw the hint of a smile on her face as she moved to the door.

"There, you're finished." Daniel patted my back and turned me so I could look in the mirror. For all of the times I'd almost been married off in the last year and a half, today was the day it would really happen. Today I was marrying Kain.

My dress was simple, elegant, and perfect for the small beach ceremony we planned. I'd decided on a long veil that hung freely from my head and disappeared into the lace of the skirt. The sleeveless flowing dress had been hemmed so that I wouldn't have to wear shoes. Small accents of blues, blacks, and golds in my jewelry represented both of our clans. My leadership pin rested on my waist, and hummed with power and approval.

I looked at my reflection, amazed at the woman staring back at me. Sure, I was only nineteen, but since ending the war with Lucian,

I'd accepted my clan leadership with pride and have worked closely with the Council and other leaders to build a new world for us all. I may have been young, but I held my own with the elders and I'd earned the respect of my kind.

Kain and I still managed our clans as one. After today, the merger would be official. Adele had offered me a seat on the Council, but after many late night discussions with Kain, I decided to postpone that invitation for a few years. I needed time to secure my leadership. Merfolk were still deciding what role the Councils would have. And Kain and I needed time with each other.

A flurry of butterflies danced in my stomach as I thought about my growing relationship with Kain. We'd been inseparable this past year. When I grieved over the loss of Brendan, he held me close and let me cry. When we needed to make tough decisions as leaders, we talked them through together and presented a unified front. It was so easy with him.

There was a part of me that was still upset for not realizing how amazing he was a long time ago. I would forever be sorry for causing him so much pain in the past, even though he promised that it didn't matter now. We only had our future to look forward to and that future would begin today.

"Earth to Eviana. Come on, they're waiting," Daniel nudged me in the side to make sure I was paying attention.

"Okay, okay." I took a deep breath and let it out slowly. "I'm ready."

Following the two of them down the stairs, we made our way through the house and out to the back deck overlooking the Pacific

Ocean. Kain and I would share our time between this house and his family's estates in Boston and Los Angeles. I had been thrilled to hear him say that he didn't want to give this place up, as it was special to him too.

Palmer waited for me outside. His wide smile and excitement were contagious. "Look at you, cuz. The most beautiful bride in the world." He kissed my cheek and held out his arm. As the closest living male relative I had, Palmer would give me away today.

Daniel and Marisol made up our wedding party. We didn't want to make it a big ordeal, especially considering all of the losses merfolk had recently endured. Despite protests from Adele and presentations from Daniel showing that he could put a spectacular wedding together, we made them promise that the affair would be small and intimate.

"Here, let's go," Marisol commanded after shoving a bouquet of flowers into my hands. The mix included roses, irises, orchids, and baby's breath. A perfect blend for a perfect summer day. Palmer and I laughed as we began our descent to the beach.

I wasn't nervous at all. For as much as I dreaded being a teenage bride not too long ago, I knew without a doubt, that this is what I wanted. Not only was it important for our clans, but I loved Kain with every cell in my body, and I *wanted* to spend the rest of my life with him. I felt like I could never get enough of his smile, his touch, or his voice. I'd realized how important he was to me a year ago, and I knew that I would never forget that again.

As we made our way toward to the group, I couldn't help but smile. Troy and his much older girlfriend were the first ones I saw. I admit I enjoyed Troy's relentless pursuit of mature women, although at least this one was a mermaid. He gave me a slight nod as we walked past, so I returned the gesture. Troy had been busy recruiting protectors to fill the ranks of both of our clans since we'd lost so many in the war. He'd become a valuable advisor and friend, and I was thankful for his consistent support.

Carissa stood next to them, grinning widely and looking like the supermodel she was. She and Palmer began dating a few months ago, and I couldn't be happier for the both of them. I thought it might be awkward between us, but not once did she give me a hard time about Kain and I being together and in fact, we'd become close friends.

Aleksey and Quinlan were next, and both of them snuck in a kiss for Daniel and Marisol as they walked past. I was surprised when Julian moved his permanent home nearby and even more amazed that he took in the two young selkies whose hearts were captured by a pair of mermaids. Their relationships wouldn't survive forever, Julian and I knew that all too well, but for now he thought it was more important to know and feel what love really was before their instincts told them otherwise.

Julian, the silent leader of the selkies, and Malcolm, who insisted on being here today, were both now a permanent part of our defense team. Our relationship with the selkies made other clan leaders uneasy, but no one protested. Especially after they saw their work in the Bahamas. Both men greeted me with a big smile and bright green eyes that would forever pierce my soul. I'd loved the selkies for such a long time, it made me whole knowing that I could keep them in my life.

And speaking of uncomfortable relationships, Isabel and Abhainn managed to come to the ceremony. The ratchets, sprites, and other creatures like the nereid's came out of hiding after the merfolk assured them we'd keep their locations a secret. They weren't without caution, and demanded several promises that included a vow that water control would never be used against them and in return, they would assist with the merfolk affairs which required their specialized skills. Mostly that meant death and destruction, but Kain and I continued to meet with Abhainn to work on our water abilities and just have a conversation with a friend. He was blissfully happy with Isabel, and it was my understanding that she'd secured her role as queen. They had a home on some secluded island in the tropics, which I understood was protected by an army of sprites.

When we reached the end of the small crowd, my heart fluttered. Kain looked amazing, and the way the sun highlighted his blond hair and tall frame, sent shivers through my body. Like I said, I couldn't get enough.

"You look beautiful," he murmured and I melted. Grabbing his hand, we let the ceremony begin. I remembered saying words and hearing him recite them back, but I couldn't seem to feel anything else except for our kiss. The moment Kain's mother pronounced us husband and wife, I jumped into his arms.

Kain laughed while we kissed, yet his lips were just as eager as mine. In the past year, we'd shared many kisses and stolen moments. He moved into my house permanently six months ago, and we spent almost every waking moment together when not called away by the responsibility of our leadership. I'd learned that he doesn't like to fold clothes, and he knew that I hated doing the dishes. He teased Marisol constantly, much to her amusement, and I was able to fall asleep in his arms every night.

The kiss lasted long enough for our friends and family to start making rude noises. We laughed but I knew this wouldn't be the last of it. A couple of weeks ago, we'd taken that final step in our relationship, creating the intimacy we'd both wanted from each other for so long. He was mine in every sense of the word and I was his. Forever.

"Are you ready?" Kain breathed in my ear, sending chills down through my toes. I nodded just before he scooped me up into his arms and ran toward the surf.

Everyone cheered as we crashed through the waves until Kain stood waist deep in the water. I couldn't stop smiling when he turned me around so that I could toss the bouquet of flowers to beach. It was even more amusing when Troy's girlfriend caught it and threw her arms around her man. The terrified look on his face was priceless.

I waved while Kain walked deeper into the sea so that we could change. My legs transitioned into a tail before I was submerged.

"Show off," he teased and then tossed me into the water. I quickly swam back to him to in time to see his pants float away toward the shore and his jacket fly through the air. He wrapped his arms around my waist, pulling me close. "I love you," he said before covering my mouth in his.

I love you, too, I thought as I let the warmth of his lips and the comfort of the sea embrace me.

Other Titles Now Available

Promises - Book One of The Syrenka Series

"Couldn't put it down."

"The storyline drew me in immediately."

"Plenty of twists and turns to keep you reading."

"Great characters and an intriguing storyline."

"...had me on the edge of my seat."

Betrayal - Book Two of The Syrenka Series

"Another great adventure."

"Betrayal is even better..."

"Swept me up from the get go."

"Amber does it again..."

About the Author

Amber Garr spends her days conducting scientific experiments and wondering if her next door neighbor is secretly a vampire. Born in Pennsylvania, she lives in Florida with her husband and their furry kids. Her childhood imaginary friend was a witch, Halloween is sacred, and she is certain that she has a supernatural sense of smell. She writes both adult and young adult urban fantasies and when not obsessing over the unknown, she can be found dancing, reading, or enjoying a good movie.

Coming Soon

Touching Evil – A Leila Marx Novel

Connect with Amber Garr Online:

www.ambergarr.com

http://ambergarr.blogspot.com

www.facebook.com – Author Page: Amber Garr

Looking for more?

If you enjoyed The Syrenka Series, then check out

Symbol of Hope Series

The fate of the gods lies in the hands
of one teenage girl.

Visit:

www.marisetteburgess.com

Available on Amazon, B&N, Kindle, and Nook

Printed in Great Britain
by Amazon.co.uk, Ltd.,
Marston Gate.